The Naked Son

C000137917

Mandla Langa, born in Durban 1950, grew up in KwaMashu township, and studied for a BA at the University of Fort Hare. After being arrested in 1976 he spent 101 days in prison on a charge of trying to leave the country without a permit. He was sentenced, skipped bail, and went into exile in Botswana.

He has participated in various arts programmes and conferences throughout Africa and elsewhere, and has lived in Botswana, Lesotho, Maputo, Angola, where he did MK military training, Zambia, Budapest and London. In 1980 he won the *Drum* short story contest for 'The Dead Men Who Lost Their Bones' and in 1991 he was awarded the Arts Council of Great Britain Bursary for creative writing, the first for a South African.

He has held various ANC posts abroad, such as Cultural Representative in UK and Western Europe. Recently he has been Vice-Chairperson of the successful africa95 Exhibition in London and he is a weekly columnist on the magazine *New Nation*. He is now convenor of the task group on government communications.

Two of his works have been published, *Tenderness of Blood* (Zimbabwe Publishing House, 1987), and *A Rainbow on a Paper Sky* (Kliptown Books, London, 1989), and he is currently producing a 13-part series of South African short stories for TV.

THE
NAKED SONG

and other stories

Mandla Langa

Africasouth New Writing

DAVID PHILIP
Cape Town & Johannesburg

First published in southern Africa 1996 in Africasouth New Writing
by David Philip Publishers (Pty) Ltd, 208 Werdmuller Centre,
Newry Street, Claremont, 7700, South Africa

ISBN 0-86486-313-6

DTP conversion by Alison Hartman
Printed by Clyson Printers (Pty) Ltd
11th Avenue, Maitland
7405, Cape

Contents

Acknowledgements

Acknowledgements are due to the following sources in which the stories listed first appeared:

'The Dead Men Who Lost Their Bones' (*Drum* magazine, 9 October 1980).

'Chukwa': *Colours of a New Day: Writing for South Africa*, edited by Sarah Lefanu and Stephen Hayward (Ravan Press, Johannesburg, 1990).

'Zizi': *The Junky's Christmas and Other Yuletide Stories*, edited by Elisa Segrave (Serpent's Tail, London, 1994).

'Proud Flesh': *Soho Square 5*, edited by Steve Kromberg and James Ogude (Bloomsbury, London, 1992).

The Dead Men
Who Lost Their Bones

They call me Clementine, here, although that is not my real name; but since I don't own a single thing here – the drab grey tunics and dresses I put on and, come to that, even myself – it does not matter any more. A lot of things have ceased to matter.

My twin sister, Benedicta (and that is not her real name, either) is here with me. This is a home that is something between a reform school and an orphanage. There are some pretty tough kids here: and the sisters are quick to punish for infringements like wetting the bed or using bad language.

Benedicta and I are sixteen years old this year, and it is close to Christmas. This place is pleasant, though, despite the unexpected punishments. Everyone (the sisters, that is) seems to be fighting a war to make us forget what happened in the past, the events that brought us here.

Many other children here have many terrible tales to tell. We eat a lot, more, in fact, than back home, but Benedicta and I are increasingly – daily – getting thinner and thinner. I guess food can never be a substitute for what the spirit hankers after. It is all very simple: we miss our parents.

I can't understand why this knowledge escapes the sisters and the Matron especially, since they are holy and knowledge-able and highly cultured people.

It was Papa who went first; Mama didn't die in the way that people die and are made one with the groaning earth. When she lost her baby – I understood this much, much later – to the shock of Papa's death, all light left her eyes; she would stare and stare and stare at the walls of our homestead. The social workers came and took her to a place for people who can no longer be responsible for their actions. Her mind had taken the long, returnless journey into the very jaws of oblivion.

It was the social workers' idea to bring us here.

Someone said that we sanctify and immortalise things by giving them words and names. There are words, now, I am forced to utter – usually in the loneliness of my bed, in the snarling silence of the midnight hour. Words like 'Mama', 'Papa', 'our house'. Our house, in reality, belonged to Meneer Gert Visser. He was a farmer, and my father – in fact, all of us, at one time or the other – worked for him. It was a beautiful farm. Mevrou Visser was a kindly woman with hair the colour of ripe orange rinds and eyes as blue and opaque as cut glass. She experimented with all kinds of plants, this remarkable woman, surprising us by dirtying her hands, digging the black earth, planting such things as flowers: zinnias, chrysanthemums; and exotic and unheard of foods like okra and plantains.

There were always bees hovering around the flowers, hovering angrily around her, so that bees and Mevrou Visser somehow get confused in my mind.

We had a job, my sister and I, to water the growing things, keeping away from the bees, early in the morning before undertaking the long trek to school, and late in the afternoon after the sun had made its silent but reluctant farewell.

Mother's chores revolved mainly around making sure that her family – and the Visser family – were kept well fed. She also cleaned their house.

It was a big house, painted white; the whole homestead was surrounded by a high, barbed-wire fence. This, I was told, was to keep dangerous animals from sneaking in during the evenings and killing the calves, lambs and kids.

Sometimes Baas Visser, as he was known, came into the farm with a squad of black men in chains. They would be given sacks to wear and would toil the whole day under the broiling sun in the fields that certainly looked endless, planting or reaping. These were bad men, I was told, and deserved to be sjambokked – as usually happened to one or two particularly hardened cases – and had a white prison guard riding a horse between the mielie rows, supervising them.

2

The Dead Men Who Lost Their Bones

The guard never forgot his rifle and his sjambok. I never forgot the eyes of the condemned men. At sundown they were chained – the way my father chained a span of oxen – and huddled together in a barn.

Mother didn't like her job; she hated the farm. She was heavy with child, so I guess she tired very easily. She carped a lot because Papa never seemed to do anything all day long except act as gun carrier for Baas Visser when they went hunting.

My father was perhaps the most handsome man I have ever seen. Whether he was in tattered overalls or his Sunday best, he managed – God knows how, because I knew how harried he must have been – to look as unruffled as ever. He had that detached air of someone perpetually preoccupied, someone wrestling with something deep and unutterably strangling. He must have loved Mama very much.

That one evening, for instance, Papa was on the verandah, cleaning his master's guns. To me, they looked like the rifle that was so much part of the guard who strutted arrogantly, on horseback.

In our little dining-room, the table was set.

'Go call your father,' Mama said. 'There's some warm water in the basin for him to wash his hands.'

I rushed outside. 'Papa?' I called. He looked up at me; there was a pale moon shining that evening, drenching the deserted farm, investing it with a cold pallor. The moonlight caught my father's face, filling his eyes with dancing things.

'Yes, Tee?' Papa always called me Tee.

'Mama says to come in. Food is ready.' I watched his hands as he cradled the barrels of the guns; his hands were shiny with oil. He picked up some waste cloth and wiped his hands. He went to the basin and soaped his hands. Cleansed after this ablution that was almost a ritual, he went into the house. Already seated at the table, Mama said, 'Love, I've always said I don't want you cleaning those awful guns around the house.' She was not really angry. She was tired.

'Aw, ma,' Papa said, sitting down beside Benedicta, 'where do you expect me to clean them – in the barn?' He shovelled a spoonful of gravy-soaked pap into his mouth. He chewed

3

absent-mindedly.

'I don't care where you do it,' Mama said, not to be outdone. 'I don't care. You could clean those guns sitting in Mevrou's flower-bed for all I care.'

'Now, wouldn't that be something?' Papa said, smiling. Then he turned to Benedicta. 'And how was my little girl's school-day today?'

'It was all right, Papa,' Benedicta said. 'We've got a new teacher from the Boland. She was introduced during the assembly time.' There was something bubbling in Benedicta's voice, an anticipation. 'And when asked to say something, she told us to pray for this troubled country – and for the Prime Minister.'

Papa laughed, but it was the choked, mirthless laughter that was hollow and infinitely mocking. 'Well,' he said, 'if you ask me, the white people here had better pray for *their* country. As for *their* Prime Minister, he'll soon know better than to run a country as if it were a taxi service.'

Mama's face was grave, indecipherable. 'Let's just please eat,' she commanded. We ate in silence for some time. Papa let his spoon drop on his plate, the sound surprisingly loud and jarring.

'You know,' Papa said, 'I figure someday very soon we're going to have to leave this farm. I'm up to here with the way things are happening around here.' There was a grating tone in Papa's voice; it had thickened considerably.

'What has happened now?' Mama asked, laying her spoon on the plate before her. Was there something like fear in her voice? *'Kwenzenjani manje, baba wabantwanami?* – what has happened now, father of my children?' She poured some coffee into thick mugs.

'You know,' Papa said, 'since Baas Visser got that stupid Skotnes boy to take care of the culling and dipping of cattle, nothing has ever gone right. That boy carries on like a regular slave-driver. I have never liked him, anyway, with a face like the underbelly of a crocodile. He calls those men from prison *kaffirs*. Kaffir this, kaffir that!' He looked at his coffee mug as though the dark, swirling beverage was the solution to a deep and impenetrable secret.

'Today we drove to the hardware store to get the plough-share sharpened. On the way we saw a big snake crossing the road, leisurely. It must have been a rinkhals, and you know how dangerous that type is. I thought that the Skotnes boy would wait until the snake had slithered into the grass, or even swerve to avoid it. You think he'd do the sensible thing? But no. He swerved to run over the snake. I don't know whether he suc-ceeded in hitting it or not, but that doesn't matter, you just don't do a damnfool thing like that with a rinkhals, or with *any* snake, for that matter. You just don't fool around with a snake, doesn't this boy have some sense!

'And, then, you know what happened?' We all knew that Papa was not waiting for an answer. He took out his pipe from the bib of the overalls and filled it; he used a piece of paper to burn the tobacco from the candle flame. There was a stertorous sound as he sucked at his pipe until the tobacco was burning evenly.

'Just when that no-good fool tried to hit the snake,' Papa went on, 'the van conked out. Kaput. And' – here Papa's voice thick-ened with rage – 'he said I must get out and push. I said, "What?" He said, "Get out and push the blerry van." I looked at him in disbelief. "You mean I must get out and push the van after you've tried to hit a snake, do you think I'm *crazy*?" He said, "Boy, get out and push the blerry van," and I said, "You're out of your blerry mind," and he got so angry – his face so red – that he balled his fists and I could see that he was ready to strike me. And I said, "White boy, just try that once and you'll see the eyes of a worm, I'm not the one who bought you this scrap." I think he saw it in my eyes that I would kill him then and there.

After much tinkering with the ignition and the accelerator, the car jumped forward. We got to the hardware store and left the ploughshare there. When he dropped me off here, on our return, he said he'd certainly report me to Baas Visser. I told him to report me to the *Volksblad*, it wouldn't turn a hair on my head.'

Even at that age, I knew there was a certain code – unspoken and unwritten – between a master and a servant who had served him for a long time. I knew that Papa had nothing to fear from the Skotnes boy; Baas Visser, if he were to be told of Papa's in-subordination, would simply ooh-aah, but nothing would come of it. The master and the servant are connected by an umbilical cord that would put both men at the gates of Hell were it to be severed.

That night we helped Mama with the dishes; Mama made the usual evening prayer. Whether by omission or design, we did not pray for the Prime Minister and the sons and daughters of the masters of the land.

The story gets increasingly hard to tell from here.

I remember that Benedicta and I came back from school and found Mama looking grave and troubled. I felt that there was something terribly wrong. I don't know how I felt this, but then this is one of the things that gets terribly hard to explain. I felt menace hanging over the air like a pall; the first thought that came to me was, *Where's Papa*? My trepidation was heightened by the presence of other people – some I'd never seen before – from the other houses on the farm. What was even more frightening was the fact that people – these strangers – were comforting Mama, saying words like, 'Don't fret, now, everything will be all right.'

For a moment we all thought that everything would be all right when Papa burst into the house, his normally ragged overalls looking as though he had been locked in a life-and-death struggle with a particularly ravenous man-eating beast. His eyes – my father's eyes – held the same expression I'd seen on the condemned faces of the manacled men in sacks.

Before Papa could say anything, in that confused babel of voices, I rushed to him and clasped him around the knees in a grip I had a feeling that even death could not undo. Slowly, wearily, my father sat down and I sat on his lap. Benedicta, her hands on his chair, looked up at the people in the room, her eyes as eloquent as the ages.

'What happened?' This was asked by someone I didn't see; it could have been Mama. But, then, my mother – who certainly knew that our normally unflappable father was at that very moment being menaced by something more consuming, more unspeakable and more ravaging than the most roaring inferno

– could not have asked anything. She was beyond questioning.

Before Papa could answer, there was the barking of dogs. Boots crunched on the gravel outside, and three policemen entered without knocking. The silence that followed their entry was more deafening than the wailing of a thousand alley cats. Two of the policemen were white; the third one, an African, looked like Thembi's father. Thembi sat next to me in class.

'Wie's Simeon Ngozi?' This was asked by one of the white policemen. I looked at him, his peaked cap, the carefully creased and laundered serge uniform, the shining holster and the brown boots. I looked at the faces of the white policemen – their cold blue eyes and thin bloodless lips – as they looked at all of us, their eyes boring into ours as though trying to break an ancient, indecipherable coded message.

My father stood up. He didn't say anything.

'Jy's Simeon Ngozi?' another disembodied voice asked. Papa nodded.

The black policeman took out a pair of handcuffs. The silver handcuffs looked strange in the black hands of the black man; the jagged edges danced cruelly in the dim light of the candle; it was as though the edges were live things, with a life of their own. *'Wag so 'n bietjie, Ngobese* – wait a minute,' one of the policemen admonished, laying a restraining, pinkish-brown hand on Ngobese's eager wrist. Ngobese, thoroughly chastised, cringed, *'Ek soek die man moet ons sê wat het regtig aangegaan* – I want this man to tell us what really happened.' There was something menacingly conciliatory about the policeman's demeanour. This, somehow, was more sinister than if the man had acted outright hostile.

'I left this morning,' Papa began, his voice cracking, weary, weary, 'with Baas Visser to our usual hunting spot in the mountain. It is very rocky, this hunting spot, and full of treacherous precipices. "We have to be careful Baas," I told the Baas; but then' – there was something immeasurably sad and wry that flickered across Papa's face – 'but, then, he told me he had been hunting on these grounds since he was this high.'

Papa was silent. He swallowed something that must have tasted like the bitterest herb. 'And then we saw a bush buck

7

darting out of a thicket into a clearing in the woods. I gave him his .303, and he told me that the bush buck would be heading our way. It seems like something startled it, for it soon bolted right back into the woods, some distance away.

'Baas Visser motioned for me to be as stealthy as possible and try to approach our quarry from the other end, out of the wind. He went straight for it, keeping to the left. I got round the thicket and he went his way. I could not see him, then, the place is dense. After a moment, I heard the loud crack of the rifle, then there was silence, then there was a scream.'

There was a loud wailing outside and a thoroughly dishevelled Mevrou Visser came into the house, screaming, *'Waar's my man? Waar's my man?'* and the two white policemen – who were certainly the only reassuring faces Mevrou Visser saw – held her, with great tenderness. The black policeman, who would have no role in the consoling of this pathetic white woman, looked as though he was beginning to doubt the wisdom of his presence in the house.

The white policemen murmured words to Mevrou Visser. We all looked at the scenario being enacted before us: all frozen in some dreadful moment in time, the scared eyes of the neighbours, mama who looked stunned, the silently sobbing Mevrou Visser: and I had a feeling that this was just another nightmare. We would all wake up tomorrow and talk about it; everything was going to be all right.

It became a nightmare. The policemen handcuffed my father, his face a mask of triumphant mockery, and steered him out of the house into the waiting Land Rover. (This is not exactly an arrest; we just want him to show us the spot, all right?) All right. Mama stood supporting herself on the table. Just when I was about to rush to Papa outside, I saw with the aid of the turning Land Rover's headlamps that streams of something dark were coursing down my mother's legs, down to her bare feet, becoming drops that turned into a dark puddle.

'Mama,' I screamed, 'you're bleeding!'

Mama lost the baby that night; Papa lost his life. The police came back around midnight and talked to an old woman who was watching over us because, you see, whilst Papa and the police were on their way to the mountain, mama was on her way to the hospital (some eighteen miles away) in an ox-wagon.

They – the police – said that when they went to do an inspection *in loco* – whatever that means – my father slipped and plummeted down, down the precipice. The police were convinced that the spot where my father perished was almost certainly the same spot where Baas Visser had begun his fateful journey into eternity. It was a crying shame, the police said, but such things have been known to happen, and the bodies have not been found, it's dark – so we'll see what tomorrow brings.

Tomorrow brought two coffins – a groaning weight – supported by an ox-wagon my father had helped make. There was silence that day; the wind did not blow, crickets and frogs were rendered mute, dogs put their tails between their legs, skulked away and forgot to bark at strangers.

Separate funeral services were held. Both coffins had been sealed, the police informed us, because the bodies had been too terribly mutilated in the dreadful plunges.

When Mama returned from the hospital, her womb ruined, she was no longer fit, the social workers said, to stay with us. They took her screaming, to the mental asylum called Fort Napier, in Pietermaritzburg. When they took her away, she did not look like our mother any more. They promised, the people who brought us here, that they would bring her back to us, as fit as a fiddle.

They are lying, of course. They never brought her back, they took us away instead. I am still wondering to this day, though, whether the still and broken body in the casket we had interred into the yawning, still and broken ground, really belonged to my father.

We will wait.

Chukwa

Ramses waited until the bus wheezed to an asthmatic stop before alighting. He could have jumped off some fifty yards back as the bus negotiated a slow corner along Starlite Hotel, but his gambler's instinct had warned against this. Might break something, he had thought. He had no wish to spoil his fourteenth birthday. He knew that he might have stumbled and perhaps lost his footing on the slippery asphalt, breaking his father's bottle of gin. Although he had just been paid and felt like a prince, he knew that bottle-stores were now closed, and, in shebeens, alcohol was ridiculously expensive.

He waited patiently until the bus left the stop, getting a whiff of acrid fumes issuing from the exhaust pipes, the smoke making wispy patterns in the rain. Knots of people huddled under awnings or umbrellas; a group of uniformed schoolchildren sought refuge in the corrugated-iron structure which could have been designed by someone with the Seven Dwarfs in mind. Ramses watched them getting soaked. He had never been to school; all he knew about the world of reading and writing came from Chukwa. She had taught him everything. She despised schools and thought that teachers and students were living in an unreal world.

Vehicles large and small careened past, some mischievous drivers splashing water on people unfortunate enough to be within range. Ramses watched the cars carefully, scrutinising each face. He knew that his father had many friends who gave him lifts. Since his injury in a train accident in 1965, Green had vowed never to use the government's public transport system. This always sounded like a contradiction to Ramses because he knew – he had seen – that cars were death traps. But Green was Green, a man with style.

Ramses was happy that his father would be visiting him. The fact that the old man was given to drinking himself to a stand-still didn't dampen his spirits. What was there to complain about when he had even received a birthday card – which boy in Klaarville could make that claim? It didn't matter that this card had been used once before, the name of the original recipient blacked-out with a felt-tipped pen and his own name sprawled across, almost filling the page. It was the thought that mattered. And the barely legible message, *I'm gonna be around your house friday rams dont mess me up love*, followed by the signature that was unlike anything the boy had ever seen, Green, the last letter becoming a tail that arced above the name to connect with the first letter's descender. Green was a craftsman.

Won't mess you up, Green, Ramses thought fiercely, never! Although somewhat disappointed by his father's lack of faith, he quickly shrugged this off as something that characterised all fathers. Gruff men, ready to assume the worst. They were no different from the morning buses which tormented workers, never waiting for people, taking off unexpectedly. He loved Green with every fibre in his body and was willing to forgive him. The rest of the jokers who passed themselves off as members of the human race could go fly a collective kite for all he cared.

When the rain came down with renewed vigour, Ramses ducked into a shop. The place was full of rain refugees and general hangers-on. A radio somewhere announced the arrest of 21 people suspected of helping the Warriors; the report was followed by a song that asked people if they had ever seen the rain. The shoppers, who seemed in no particular hurry to buy anything, lounged around, their breath misting against the plate glass. There was a smell of unwashed socks, frying oil and poverty. Two young women with adult eyes sipped their cokes, elbows resting on the counter. Ramses looked at them, saw their ginger wigs and tomorrow's clothes and knew that they would soon be plying their trade around the shopping centre. He felt a depthless sadness. He wondered what it would have been like to have a sister.

He bought two packets of fish and chips, a loaf of brown bread, four Russian sausages and a bottle of Sprite. Having paid, he tried to edge his way out, the heat and the combined smells giving him a headache. He could sense the hungry eyes of some of the people boring into his back like acid. To hell with them, he thought savagely. People who didn't know how to take care of themselves deserved what they got. This was the city; it ground into fine dust whoever was unaware of its laws. Other people – the type he despised the most – looked at him with a mixture of wonderment and pity, concluding that the money in the black boy's hands had been stolen from somewhere. To hell with them, too!

He walked the dark street lined by jasmine shrubs and jaca-randa trees. As he smelled the flowering bushes, his mind went back to the early years in Zeleni. He remembered the verdant bushes that were always menacing. He used to tremble in the dark, afraid of a malevolent Indian spirit which would do unnameable things to young boys. This terror was heightened by witnessing the seasonal Hindi rituals where believers came out in their finery and walked on live coals, pierced themselves with sharp instruments or lay on spike beds. Other conjurers swallowed flames; their young children – some of whom Ramses had once known – would appear dressed in loud pastel colours that rivalled the intensity of the flames. Their chants which might have come from another world; the flatbed trucks that had been turned into floats with wild flowers and garlands that recalled wreaths and – most frightening of all – the garishly painted, grinning figure inside the small hut, the god of the Indians, which would be burnt in a consuming fire that could set the whole world ablaze; all this was accompanied by singing, and incessant chants and drumming that went on into the night. What was the meaning of it all? He had asked Chukwa about it and she had become very angry and told him that there were things he should not question.

But the other African children didn't seem awed; to them, this was just another carnival. When the procession passed on the main road to Zeleni, these children would sing and do a jig, taunting the celebrants: *Inkosi yamaNdiya Bayifak'odongeni Bayincish'ubanana Kwakhal'u-dum-dum!*

They would shriek in mock fear and scamper away when they saw the truck which contained the undying spirit. For nights on end, Ramses' dreams would be a screaming playground for gargoyles, gorgons and ghosts.

As he walked down the street, the memory of Zeleni triggered off an insupportable yearning for his mother. On most days when he felt low, Ramses would conjure up images of a young woman who wore a scarlet doek on her head; she would have strong hands and a honey-flavoured voice. He saw her outline but never her face, and this caused him immense pain. Even when he called upon all his powers of concentration, the face would forever stay in the shadows, unseen, as mysterious as a shrine. And she was always singing. He strove to catch the melody and lyrics of her song, but that, too, would be denied him.

Whenever he was sure that she had deserted him, something would happen to raise his hopes. It happened one afternoon when he was twelve years old that he accompanied Chukwa to her favourite spot on the shore where she watched boats and liners gliding on the sea *en route* to some unknown destination. They saw a woman standing alone on a clump of rocks looking at the sun which was setting in a great blood-red orb on the horizon. There was something restless and yet full of tension about her. Ramses told Chukwa that the woman should be his mother. Chukwa, knowing her friend's dreams – sometimes dreaming them herself – wordlessly agreed to follow him. The closer they got to the figure, the more convinced was Ramses that this time he had finally come to the end of his search for his mother. The same clothes, the same way of standing with her weight on her left leg, the hip pressed against a rock that jutted up like a church spire, one arm dangling, her whole pose communicating that she had come here to lose herself in dreams about the sea.

When she heard their footsteps crunching on the pebbled sand, the woman turned round. The two children saw that she was white. She stood there watching their stupefied faces in

13

silence. There was neither reproach nor welcome on her face, just a mute acceptance of that moment of encounter. Then she stretched her arms and beckoned for them to come nearer. Chukwa, who was much braver than Ramses, pulled and pushed and had him in tow by the time they reached the woman.

'What brings you here, my children?' she asked. Her voice was so low that they had to strain to hear it above the risen wind.

'We're looking for his mother,' Chukwa answered.

'Ah,' the woman said, a bit of colour returning to her cheeks. 'Did she love the sea, then?' Chukwa couldn't answer. In her own dreams, Ramses' mother was always dressed in a pink housecoat.

'I don't know,' Ramses said, having found his tongue. He felt wretched. 'I don't know.'

'Neither do I,' the woman said. 'I come from England, where they took my children, and I can't go back now.'

Ramses and Chukwa studied her face; it was a face that seemed carved out of a rare stone, hard and unyielding. It was clear that she had once been very beautiful before something with cold fingers touched her in an unknowable private moment. Was it possible that this spectre with a body as flat as a board had once experienced joy, perhaps in those months before her children were wrested away from her? Her slate-grey eyes were so full of pain and longing that the children took a step back and fell into the water – people had no right to endure so much. It was as if the woman had countenanced everything evil under the sun and her eyes were screaming for deliverance, for a chance to look upon beauty and grace, even for one moment.

Then the woman said in a girlish voice, 'Gone are the days of ruling the waves, now the black tide comes in.' Then she laughed, a long raucous exclamation that caused gulls to soar into the air. It was the loneliest sound on earth. 'You look at the sunflower plantations,' she said to herself, 'yellow and black and a green bush, maybe a field of roses redder than menstrual blood. What happens to the statues of civilisation, all those people talking about Empire and the Colossus of Rhodes and here we are now and silence reigns. Gnarled trees.'

She was no longer talking to them. The children started taking steps backwards, keeping their eyes on the woman, little fish nipping at their legs. They were convinced that she was out of her mind. The woman heard them going, but didn't turn to look at them. She merely commanded: 'Stop.' The children ran, out of the water and onto the beach, stumbling and falling, determined to escape. Having put enough distance between themselves and the woman, they stopped to catch their breath. That was when Chukwa saw an embroidered canvas bag in a clump of sedge. She picked it up and, like all children of the hungry city, searched it, looking for something to eat.

'That belongs to the woman,' Ramses said. 'How would you know?' Chukwa asked and added belligerently, 'Anyway, finders keepers.'

'I know. In my dream mama carries a bag like that. Anyway, what's inside?'

Chukwa removed her wet dress and spread it carefully on the sand. Ramses saw her little girl's breasts, the V where her legs joined the belly, a mysterious darkness that harboured unmentionable secrets. He caught his breath and felt a kind of fear that he had never experienced before.

'What are you staring at?' Chukwa demanded, throwing the bag at him, 'Empty the fokken thing!' Ramses emptied the contents of the bag on Chukwa's dress. A comb, a compact case, two sticks of lipstick which looked obscene in the near-gloom of the approaching evening, a switchblade, a half-eaten tuna sandwich in a polythene wrapper; then the children caught their breath as wads of twenty- and fifty-rand notes plop-plopped on the cheapest cloth on earth.

'What should we do?' Chukwa asked, her toughness undermined now in the real world of rands and cents. A cold gust of the wind which the inhabitants called *Ikhomazi* blew and she shivered. Ramses noticed that the blast had left a rash of goose pimples larger than kidney beans on her skin. He was also shivering, but not from cold; he was shivering from fear. 'Let's take it back to her,' he pleaded. 'But she's completely befok,' Chukwa countered, 'can't you see that?' Ramses regarded his friend as if from a great height. 'It's not our business if she's mad,' he put in stubbornly. 'It's her money and she must do whatever she wants to do with it.' Chukwa gave a grim smile. 'Maybe she'll give it to the mental hospital at Farnworth,' she said. Then she sighed and shrugged. 'Okay.'

For one long moment which seemed suspended in the air, the seaside was beset by a great calm. Where the gulls had been screaming hoarsely, and where the sea had raged and rocked, there was now a palpable quietude that was louder than a dynamite explosion in the quarries. Dusk settled like an opaque blanket, the only place giving off light was above the line where the water met the sky.

The sea resumed its viciousness when the children retraced their steps to the spot where they had last seen the woman. They saw the water lashing the rocks with anger, banging against the concrete bulwark on which rusted hooks were fastened, everything covered by lichen and barnacles. Ramses wondered where all this anger came from, hoping to catch a glimpse of the woman who had suddenly become such a major part of their lives. The woman was nowhere to be seen.

'She's gone,' Ramses said unnecessarily, his fear returning. 'Maybe she was never there in the first place,' Chukwa said. 'What shall we do with this?' Ramses asked, pointing at the money as if it were a snake of whose death people weren't really convinced. 'Let's go and count it in my shack,' Chukwa advised, 'Then we can bury it.' 'But …?' Ramses started. 'No "buts", Ramses,' Chukwa snapped. 'Let's just go. This is the world.'

The next morning was without surprises. The world that Ramses and Chukwa viewed with suspicion hadn't changed. Turbines still turned and factories still released poison through phallic chimneys. The seaside flats and hotels where white people worshipped the government of the hour still looked invincible, these castles defended by armoured guardians of colour – the reflecting windows not letting out the smells of breakfasts and perfumes, or the sounds of happy, flaxen-haired tots, or the loveless gropings on satin sheets. All this mocked the beggars and the disabled who lined the street, shouting their misfortune and affliction in hundreds of sharps and flats.

Then the children heard the newspaper vendor proclaim to the passing cars, translating in words the chilling headlines on the placard: *Sunday Tribune! Golden City Post! British Heiress Drowns! Read all about it!* The children, bonded by a secret deeper than blood, walked on, wondering about the nights when the inheritor's ghost would appear to claim her legacy.

Zizi

I am running along this beach, which has been reclaimed. The signs, once empowered to prescribe swathes of landscape for particular communities, are now down. The vegetation thrives and there is everywhere the taste of salt in the air. The muddy banks of the river which flows into the sea support bulrushes and haulms of sedge. Out of the vast, restless sea comes a blast of spume which gives an effect of something big and ineffable insinuating itself into lives of ordinary people. The aquamarine surface of the sea shimmers, changes and assumes the colours of the sun; spangled bubbles summon the memory of precious stones. There is something unreal about this scene which suggests that one is inside a many-layered dream, which peels off, like an onion, and introduces the dreamer to another experience. Armed with this knowledge that I might wake up to another illusion, I am not fooled by appearances. What is real is real. But I am also familiar with wet dreams of fulfilment in a hungry world.

This realisation that we operate without trust and expect life to be hard, and happiness to be recalled only in misery, causes me to wonder what will finally become of us. We are like orphans bereft of the head of the household, where mirrors and all the artefacts of remembrance get covered by a shroud which shields the profaned life from the nakedness of our eyes. The sea voices its neutrality, but the waves crashing against the rocks, the iridescent spray, fail to appease my personal anger. I imagine that the rage speaks to the elements. The rollers, it seems, are not so much enraged as surprised that something so sacred and dear could have been blasphemed. There are few people left who will remember what this stretch of land and water once meant to us. Most of my former friends and playmates are gone. Some of those who remained retreated into an inner world whose silence transcends the grave. They are there, but they are also not there. To try to prise them out of torpor, to wake the sleepwalker in them, is an act more desperate than indulgence in fantasies.

Because I am one of them, and I find myself going through the motions of living, I have arrogated the right to tell my story, which is also their story. But, an idea hits me. No, this is Zizi's story, and you know Zizi. He is the thing that bursts inside you, at the same time making you feel whole, as if you had a heart. Something pulses in that corner of a man's chest where such activity throbs. And you feel it won't stop, even if Zizi is pushing you to it, until you explain who he was – is – this boy, Zizi, who died in the docks.

As I run, feeling the sand subsiding beneath my toes, I marvel at the arrogance of it all. I believe I am a rational man, but, then, which ghost is not given to a little self-delusion? Zizi is unhelpful when it comes to unravelling the narrative; he knows that no one can imagine what we went through. And he can play the fool because he is dead, and death has been known to bring about great irresponsibility: people cannot touch you. Which is strange in some way, because, of the group, Zizi was the most considerate. He would say to you, *'Thuthuka* – bless you!' when you sneezed (or even when you coughed). And he would help old women with their shopping baskets from the Indian Market on Victoria Street on Saturday mornings. And they would not even say to him, 'Go away, you little scamp!' as they were wont to react to us. He was that kind of boy, very dependable. It possibly came from the fact that his one leg was shorter than the other, I cannot remember which, and he walked with a pronounced limp. We would never make fun of him, because Zizi had the strongest arms south of the Equator and could wrestle the most well-built of us to the ground. I have been hit in my days, even by big policemen, but nothing beats the morning when Zizi slapped me across the face for calling him a fool, the ringing in the ears, the stars that swam and the tears that sprang into my eyes.

It was Siza who suggested that since we were on summer holidays, and we were beginning to take an interest in girls, who were certainly noticing the rags we wore, we should get holiday jobs. The fashion in the township of KwaMashu consisted of Sta-Press trousers or Levi's jeans, Converse sneakers, Viyella button-down shirts; sometimes a black windbreaker with a ribbed collar above a BVD T-shirt. No imitations.

'There's no work, Siza,' someone complained, 'not in Durban.'

'Yes,' I supplied. 'Our fathers trudge the pavements seeking work ...'

'Don't tell us about your father.' It was Zizi. 'He's a priest. The only trudging he does is from Genesis to Malachi.'

'Still ...'

Siza snapped, 'Still nothing. Just look at us.' He sounded angry. 'Cast-offs from brothers, uncles. No self-respecting scarecrow would be seen dead in these ...' he judged himself '... rags.'

For a moment, it was as if he wanted to cry. But he was fourteen, and it wouldn't have been the right thing to do. I was also fourteen. Changes were happening in my head; some, in that distant, confused moment, in my body. When this happened to you, you realised that the pillars you had heard so much about, which, maybe, Samson shook, are still there, intact, gearing up to demonstrate, with a vengeance, that your old man was talking shit. Something curdles up in you, love, and you remember that you are your father's son.

Which was all fine. These noble notions. Who was Zizi's father? I remember him as someone I could possibly have worked at liking. Trim, dapper; Arrow shirts. He wore shoes that gleamed, and it was clear that they were patent leather, maybe Italian. Moustache flecked with assigned grey. He had a car, a Valiant, which he would rev for a while before driving off.

'He's okay, my dad. Full of things,' said Zizi. Pause, speculative. His eyes did not need to talk. 'Ma's sleeping. Feel I have to ask you to be here when we do the asking. You mind?'

'No. Fine with me.'

'Fix you sommin'? Tea? Coffee?' Then Zizi cursed. 'Know you hate all that. Coke? Seven-Up?'

'Seven-Up.'

My township, KwaMashu – which very few people want to claim – is there. I suspect that in those hidden corners in which I stuck my broad nose – and people were offended – something waited with a bated breath. Mine was a township of copses and darkness. Looking at the areas abutting the stations of KwaMashu and Tembalihle: is that not where we grew up and plotted robbing the Post Office and Sithole's supermarket? An area so full of humankind, where you hear the sound of sizzling fat-cakes, juicy sausages on a griddle, or jive to the latest tune today, baby, 'cause tomorrow it would be gone.

As a preacher's son, whatever I said, I was a victim of my parentage. I would come up with the most daring idea for mischief, but the fellows would shake their heads and roll their eyes and make me feel useless. My clothes were cast-offs from the congregations. I was an emotional case whose survival was determined by the prosperity of the believers and their weekly tithes. A pariah. This was unbearable.

My father did not come from South Africa. He had traversed the length and breadth of the northern Transvaal. Messina. Bushbuckridge. He was black, yes, but he spoke Zulu with an accent, which was not lost on my friends. My mother, understanding my bewilderment, did not fight me. She used the family to fight me. There were always, in the context of our holy, pentecostal church, rituals to redeem the sinners and bring them to the altar of the alabaster Christ.

I did not hear her, Zizi's mother, until she was upon us, speaking from behind me, in that voice.

'So,' she said, 'you elected to feed yourself, huh? Zizi?'

This is where I escape, I thought. Tongue stinging with the fizz of Seven-Up, I turned from the kitchen stool to look at her. An ordinary mother in a faded pink housecoat. Possibly sensing my intention, she brought her elbow with a thump on the table and looked at me. 'This what you being taught at home?' she asked. 'Just coming in and having a right royal time?'

'Ma …?'

'Don't you ma me, Zizi. This is stupid.' Her mouth trembled. She was the most beautiful, desirable woman I had ever seen, really. Skin like black velvet, I wanted to touch her. I realised, at that exact moment, why our country would never survive as long as it continued to lie to itself.

'Where would you find work?' She was talking to her son but I had a feeling she was addressing me. Being hopelessly in love with her, I imagined all sorts of things. But I decided to keep my mouth shut.

'The docks, Ma,' Zizi said. 'Boys are being taken on as casual labour.'

She made a sucking sound with her teeth. 'And you think you'll survive there?' She barked out, once, a harsh laugh which sounded like a sob. The sunlight washed the kitchen table and bounced against her face. She caught me looking at her, and something like a cold flame flickered in her eyes, once, twice, and disappeared. I still wonder what she thought of me. She probably divined that I was shy; maybe she concluded that I was somewhat retarded.

I was sure she had sensed me watching her on the weekly occasion when she hung the washing on the line, tossing socks and underwear like a netball player, the fabrics arcing in the piercing morning air to land on the clothesline, she was that good. Like all mothers, she had a great capacity to instil guilt in a boy.

'Do your mom and dad know about this?' This time she was talking to me.

'Yes,' I lied. Growing up in the theatre of the church creates the most accomplished liars. My mother and father would have had a seizure apiece if they had known what we were planning. I had had my fair share of beatings by my father when I forgot to water the plants or light the paraffin lamps at dusk. My response to all this was that I had to take it like a man; I felt that I deserved the punishment. What I feared most was to be thrashed by my mother.

Anyone who knows the intimate pain of carrying you for nine months – and the wrenching terror of childbirth – knows something about her issue's threshold of pain, how to turn on the screws and elicit the appropriate scream. Mothers are bad news. Which is why the teachers, when faced with a rebellious student, always used the threat: 'I will call your mother to the school.' This had the effect of bringing about a lasting peace.

Zizi's mother didn't believe me, I know this. But, when she shook her head and looked at the weeds that were rubbing their backs against her fresh maize stalks, she relented and agreed that Zizi should come with me. It could have been for any number of reasons. The streets were out there baring their teeth and flexing their muscles, ready to claim any boy. The streets swaggered in threes or fours and loitered around the *stoeps* of shops, blowing fogs of sickly sweet-smelling Durban Poison. They pursed their lips and whistled at young women and cursed old men and flashed the blade at the slightest provocation. In a small way, then, I think, Zizi's mother must have been grateful that her son was not regarded as an oddity, that he was part of the royal fellowship of something nearest to wholesome boy-hood. If she had only known.

It was just our luck that on our first day out it was raining as if the heavens had gone crazy. Durban had always been a wet city; but on this occasion, the rain seemed to be coming down not so much as a climatic necessity: it had assumed a life of its own, the same way musical notes sometimes come out of the brass bell of a trumpet to enjoy their own selves. The nights in Durban were like that, too; nights that proclaimed their own nocturnal nature, something which confounded the brightest torches.

On this wet Monday morning, we queued at the bus rank. By the time we were inside, we were soaked to the skin. The interior of the bus was overwhelmed by Jackson's cigar smoke.

He was a thin Malawian, as black as tar. It seemed that he smoked the evil-smelling cigars to irritate the women who were on their way to the madams' kitchens. They were discouraged from opening the windows because the cold air carrying icy raindrops was more unbearable than Jackson's fumigation.

'These MaNyasa,' the women would hiss, 'coming here with their strange ways!'

MaNyasa was a derogatory term used for people who came

from Malawi. If Jackson heard this, he did not let on. He puffed on, his ebony face as serene as a river. We certainly couldn't say anything to him because Jackson was our key to the shipyard construction company to which we were going.

The bus roared on, picking up passengers at every stop until it was so packed that breathing was difficult; an auntie dared slide the window open to let in respirable air. We passed the brace of industrial buildings near The Point; a few feet to the left rose the grim greyness of The Point prison, its walls as sturdy as a fortress. We followed Jackson out two stops farther up. He led us to a clearing where a barracks-style prefabricated building stood forlornly. He knocked on the door, took off his hat and went in.

'What do you think will happen?' I asked.

'We'll see,' Siza said. 'Just don't get nervous. Jackson knows what he's doing.'

'Water is seeping in through my shoes,' I complained.

'Bugger the water,' Siza said. He was nervous despite the show of bravado.

A few minutes later, Jackson came out, followed by two white men in hard hats. One was big with a beer belly; his companion was as thin as a rake, but there was something about them, the way they regarded each other, which made them seem like brothers. The thin one cleared his throat. My father always cleared his throat before making a long speech.

'My boys,' he said, 'I don't know what Jackson has been telling you. Be that as it may, we are here to work. I'm taking you to the docks, we are going to sweat there, make no mistake. You'll be paid hourly. If you work hard, we'll get along fine. If you don't, you'll soon know why men have given me a certain nickname.'

A white van with the company name stencilled on the side panels pulled up. We were waved into the back. Jackson sat in the cab with the thin white man and an African driver in blue-denim overalls. We could see traffic along Congella, the brownstone building of the Electricity Supply Commission, the smoke billowing from the twin towers of the Hulletts sugar company.

24

To the right, people were already queuing up to enter the King Edward VIII Hospital. We were headed for Mobeni.

'What is his nickname?' I asked.

'People call him *Mlom'wengwenya* – the mouth of the croco-dile.' Zizi seemed to know everything.

'I wonder why he's got a name like that.'

'You'll have enough time to find out,' Siza said. 'In the mean-time why don't you all shut up, maybe we can hear what they're cooking up in front.'

We pricked up our ears but could hear little above the roar of the traffic and the bone-rattling bumps as the wheels hit the pot-holes. Soon enough we were passing through Clairwood, the gum-trees and wattles paving the road, bougainvillaea and jasmine drooping in the rain. Indian and Coloured people milled about, some ducking the downpour, throwing themselves un-der bus shelters. Some schoolchildren in uniform emerged from the houses, satchels knocking against young, bobby-soxed legs and Bata shoes. The settlements were waking up.

We reached the industrial site at 6.45 a.m. Men were already preparing themselves for work, stripping off their ragged street clothes to put on even more ragged overalls. Sandblasting equip-ment began to whirr; then a powerfully built man, whose torso glistened with perspiration and rain, started the siren. It was one of the loudest sounds I had ever heard.

We were parcelled off to the dry dock where we climbed down the long steel ladder riveted to the wall. Down below was sludge which we were required to shovel into a big bucket. This was in turn winched up and out and emptied. Then it was lowered down and the cycle began again.

Crocodile's corpulent friend called us out around eleven o'clock. We were then assigned to the shipyard detail. Here we were installed on suspended planks, to apply carmine indus-trial coating on ship plates. The water, some thirty feet below, was dirty; it swirled with rotting timber and the detritus of in-dustry. High above us, some other casual labourers were chip-ping paint off the deck, using hammers, the din deafening. Some-one had brought a radio; the FM station was loud with Christ-mas carols, accompanied by the voice of the announcer telling us about the goodness of our leaders during whose benevolent watch we were nearing the commemoration of Christ's birthday.

The siren signalling lunch sounded and we made our way to the steady ground at the industrial site. The three of us crept under a trailer and munched our peanut-butter sandwiches and washed them down with tepid tea from Zizi's flask. I was already dog-tired; my two friends weren't faring any better. I looked out at the sea, which was grey, and you couldn't see where it ended and the sky started. A lone liner cruised slowly across the water; its sight brought about a yearning that was almost insupportable. I wished we had been born elsewhere in different circumstances, where we wouldn't have to work so hard just to buy Christmas clothes. I wished that my father were rich and owned an Oldsmobile in which he would take us to the beach on Sundays. Siza, who had been lying on his back, staring at the trailer's chassis, suddenly turned and rested on his elbows.

'What in hell are we doing here?' he asked.

'It was all your idea,' I said. 'Wasn't it?'

'Stop this bickering,' Zizi said. Then he seemed to consider. 'I hear say that they'll give us a bit extra come Christmas week.'

'Says who?' I asked.

'Jackson. He got it from Crocodile.'

'I'll be damned if I'm setting foot here tomorrow,' Siza swore. 'What kind of place is this? You know that guy who starts the siren? He's deaf and dumb. That explains why he works like a madman.'

'Don't know about you fellows,' Zizi says. 'But I have to come back. Again and again.'

This made Siza and me a little ashamed because we were bigger and healthier than Zizi. Here he was now, making us seem like whingeing ninnies. I thought of challenging Siza on his statement which suggested that deaf and dumb people were mules. But before I could advance an argument, the siren screamed once, twice; the lunch period was over and we were back to our assigned posts.

The day passed and we were handed our pay. We took the

bus home after establishing that we would come back the next day. Zizi had won. We all slept all the way in the bus and were woken up by Jackson near our stop. 'See you tigers tomorrow.' He disappeared into a shebeen.

We dragged ourselves to the bus stop the following morning, and the day after, for one week. The routine was beginning to make sense. We could even play tricks on Jackson and Crocodile. Just when everything was becoming familiar, we were transferred to cleaning the ship's engine.

Meanwhile, on the beach, this life of exertion becomes enjoyable; the air thickens and I feel the strain in my calves as the water and sand pull at my feet. People pass, some are running, like me, but most of them content themselves with walking and enjoying the morning on the seaside. Someone passes, his radio, or what the kids nowadays call the boom-box, blasts loud soul music, Arthur Conley, I think. There is something sorrowful and optimistic about the singer's voice. It is the voice of someone familiar with pain. For me it is a balm. I run on. And as I follow the footprints of an earlier walker, I see the celebrants baptising the believers in the water; a knot of robed people sing and beat on drums. There is a slower tempo beneath the spiritual, and beneath it the moaning of a woman, someone in the throes of a nameless peril, and I remember Zizi when he screamed.

The engine room was unlike others I had seen in factories where I delivered messages to some members of my father's church. The boilers were larger but cleaner here; the flames behind glass panels convinced me that they were not using coal for fuel. Since the ship was stationary, the furnaces and boilers were merely for providing heating for the cabins and perhaps hot water for the showers used by the Belgian crew on the upper decks. We were issued with miners' hats strapped with little torches on the front, well-worn gloves, and buckets in which swirled a corrosive detergent. Our task was simply to follow a narrow chamber and scoop the grease from the machinery. The heat inside was intense and I could actually feel heat rash covering the exposed areas of my body. It was filthy work and the odour of the detergent, which must have been highly inflammable, made it feel dangerous.

Since Zizi was slighter in build, he was required to lead us. We crawled on our bellies and slid through vertical and horizontal channels, shovelling the goo into the buckets with our hands. My torch went out and I was plunged into a carbon darkness, something deeper than the darkness experienced when you shut your eyes tight at night. I followed what I thought was the route which Zizi had taken. Also, I could not hear Siza, who was supposed to be behind me. Terror clawed at me. I whispered, 'Zizi?' My voice bounced back at me. I removed the gloves and tried to feel my way about, and my hand capsized the bucket. The liquid splashed against the floor and into my eyes. I screamed once as my eyes burnt; the scream, even when I had stopped, continued ringing, a sound that was louder than the lunch-time siren. Zizi was screaming at the top of his voice.

I do not know to this day how I made my way out. But I do remember sitting on the deck, retching, while Siza thumped my shoulders, asking what had happened. Where was Zizi? In that almost tranquil moment, there was an urgent throbbing in my temples as if my head would burst open like an over-ripe watermelon. A man in a captain's uniform was gesturing animatedly as he talked to Crocodile, who seemed to have lost his characteristic swagger. A siren sounded, but this time it was not jarring; it carried a certain sad and valedictory tone which accentuated the stillness of the afternoon. Some birds soared above us and left a silver after-image of themselves as they dived into the water.

After what seemed like an eternity, Siza came up from behind and stroked my cheek with a greasy hand. I turned to look up at him and it was in his face that I read what had happened.

'He's dead, isn't he?' I asked.

'Yes,' Siza said. 'He was trapped in the propeller shaft and they couldn't haul him out.'

There was a wildness about his movements which contrasted strangely with the serenity in his eyes. I held his gaze before my eyes were drawn to the dull gleam of the captain's polished shoe leather. Set alongside these were Crocodile's scuffed *velskoene*. The two men were still arguing some point heatedly when I stood up and lunged at Crocodile, beating him about the face, screaming, until hands pulled me back and pinioned me against the railing.

We buried Zizi on Christmas Eve in the grounds of the new cemetery in KwaMashu. Some children from our class attended, their faces transformed by their inability to comprehend what had happened. Zizi's mother and father stood over the mound, bonded by the tragedy but seeming more isolated from each other than ever before. When Zizi's mother raised her face to look at the sun, I understood the terrible beauty of bereavement.

I heard later that the construction company paid them vast sums of money. Zizi's parents separated, the mother settling somewhere else, in the city. Zizi's father drifted from one woman to another; he changed cars, but he had lost his township hipster strut. Much later, he hit the bottle with a vengeance and nearly got killed in a car crash. Eventually, he also moved from KwaMashu and I heard that he was in Clermont Township, running taxis.

Siza and I found that we had nothing in common. Our friend's death had also killed the tenuous link between us. He left school and worked as a bus conductor; on the rare occasion I bumped into him, he looked sadder and heavier and sounded infinitely coarser. I knew that he would in time join some Holy Roller sect, and scale even higher reaches of self-delusion.

It was when we were writing our matriculation exams that I was visited by Zizi. I was struggling with a Biology paper trying to figure out how to label a cross-section of the eye. Zizi pulled up a chair and sat down beside me. He had put on weight in death and his face glowed as if he were using skin-lightening creams. He smiled as he handed me a piece of paper where the drawing was clearly labelled. I must have been so surprised that I cried out.

The invigilator gave me a disapproving look and threatened to throw me out. 'Don't panic,' Zizi whispered. 'Here,' he said, sliding a white envelope under my question papers. 'This is for Ma. The address is written outside. Tell her I'm okay.' He looked at me and I saw that his eyes were full of unexpressed desires. When I next looked he was gone.

That afternoon I took a bus to Sycamore Road in town. I found the address without difficulty. Zizi's mother was there, in a maid's pink uniform. She looked at me with neither welcome nor hostility, just a bland acceptance of something inevitable. She took the envelope and thanked me politely. When I started to ask her a question, she placed a forefinger against my lips. I caught the smell of Lifebuoy soap and fresh linen. Then she closed the door firmly against my face.

I am tired now but I still punish myself. I do a U-turn and head back to where I started. The baptism is still going on. As I run, I remember all the people, all the faces we confronted in our attempts to confront ourselves. There were those children with whom I left in 1976 after the slaughter in Soweto. Running on this beach I recall how we resolved to return and claim what was ours. In all that time in unfamiliar lands where I sought a salve in the arms of strangers, I hankered after unravelling the mystery of Zizi's death and re-appearance. I asked myself many questions, had I imagined it, had it all been conjured up by a feverish mind.

I see the woman, freshly emerged from the water, holding onto the arms of the preacher. Zizi's mother looks older and more frail. Dressed in white robes she seems more wraithlike than her undead son. She raises her eyes, possibly to look at the sky for signs of her living god, and they meet mine. They are eyes that have watched so many rise, so many stagger and go under. They have borne witness to everything: from the acres in the plantations to the miles of scrubbed kitchen floors; the hundreds of thousands of little sons and daughters of the masters of the land, understanding love as they nestle in the bosoms of despised mamas. They will be there, these eyes, to remind us of our folly when we stagger, here, on the horizon, now in this stammering season and they will teach us the innocence of violence and the value of miracles.

I do not say anything. The sand beckons, and the believers continue their ceremony of endurance.

Proud Flesh

It was in the last week of November that the papers reported the case of an Oudtshoorn farmer who had killed a black labourer. The dead man, known as Makgatho, was suspected of stealing a chicken. In a rage, the farmer had bludgeoned him to death. 'It's what these people do,' the farmer said in his defence. He was not going to repent. It was also the week when eight people, five men and three women were found shot and hacked to death near the KwaMashu railway station. The bodies, in conformity with the universally accepted rule that corpses should be as inelegant as possible, were depersonalised by cameras and eyes that had witnessed their nakedness. They showed signs of torture: cigarette burns and weals caused by sjamboks. Evidently, the beatings, the torture and the execution had been committed elsewhere before the bodies were dumped here. There was no apparent motive – there never was – except that all were known to have connections with the ANC. The report accompanying the picture listed the names of the dead, an inventory of horror.

Blade read the name of Khaya Ngidi. Something about the name made him sit up. His mind, befuddled by long nights in the shebeen after a gig at the Crazy Horse nightclub, was jolted by this discovery. He had known Khaya at Pango where he had been one of the section commanders; then Khaya had left for Lusaka where he had worked with ordnance before disappearing. How is it possible that a trained man like that could have been caught unawares? Blade knew that many such questions would remain unanswered for a long time.

He washed and dressed. Looking in the mirror, he encountered a stranger. His eyes were bloodshot; there was a bruise above the left eye. What happened? He thought of going to ask Lungi who was pottering around sullenly in the kitchen. He knew she must be angry because he couldn't remember how he had got back. He imagined people carrying him from the car, depositing him, like a sack of meat rations from a Lusaka butchery, on the front stoep, knocking and leaving hastily to avoid Lungi's interrogation. She had a sharp tongue, that one, Blade thought, marvelling at her spunk but at the same time sickened by his dependence on her. What has become of us? he wondered.

In was in her eyes that he saw how thoroughly condemned he was. They were puffed and red from crying. This was somehow unlike Lungi, who was as tough as nails; but, he knew, he had penetrated her shell and was able to touch those parts she had protected with her tongue and toughness. *She makes love just like a woman,* he remembered lines from an unforgettable song, *and she breaks down just like a little girl.*

He came up to her and she turned her back and concentrated on cleaning the stove, the kettle boiling on a side plate, the hiss of the steam filling the kitchen. Somewhere in the house a radio played a song that celebrated passion.

Even the president needs passion, someone sang and Blade remembered a president he had known and respected and would have died for if the opportunity had been there. But that was a long time ago. So much had happened and he knew he had changed and been changed by his re-entry into his country. He touched Lungi's shoulder, felt the thin silky fabric of her nightgown, and something knotted up in his stomach.

'I am sorry, Lungi,' he began.

She turned round to face him, the wet face looking as unfamiliar as a stranger's; her eyes searched his in an attempt to come to the bottom of the mystery of what had bonded them together in the first place. He had known how easy it was for lovers to become, at some snarling hour, total strangers. What mystified him was the knowledge that people organised liaisons with the knowledge of the probable moment of parting always at the back of the mind. Or, to be more precise, that was

how he approached relationships. This realisation always filled
him with sadness because he knew that he was beyond the point
of feeling. Throughout life, he had been going through the motions. So, when she turned to look at him like that, with those
wounded eyes, he wondered whether he really didn't hate
women.

'Why do you do such things?' Lungi asked. It was a question
that came with the ease – and difficulty – of having been repeated over and over until it had become the only question
which could be the basis of their partnership. 'Do you want to
leave?' she asked.

'What day is it?' he asked.

'Friday.' Lungi continued looking at him, possibly trying to
find in his face some recognisable pieces which could be glued
together to rebuild their shattered lives. 'If you want to leave,'
she said, 'feel free. It's cool with me.'

What did I do . . . last night?'

'You don't want to know.'

'Seriously. Tell me.'

'Where should I start?' Lungi asked. 'The fight at Nokwe's
spot? How you groped Sis Patty and boasted that you're the
Playboy of the Western world? Or how you were chucked out
when you picked a fight with Alf? Or the wet sheets in the ham-
per? Should I go on?' He shook his head. 'No.' Sighing, feeling
that he wouldn't be able to face a single soul outside, he sat on
the chair and looked at the flies on the lace curtains.

'The problem here', Lungi said, 'is that we won't know what
has happened to you. You know that for many of us a returned
exile is something like a king. We look up to them because they
have been outside this stinking mess. And they have been fighting. Young people look up to you, their brilliant light. What do
you think happens when they see a drunk pissing all over himself? Do they feel that all this was worth it?'

'No.'

'Of course not.' Lungi rinsed her hands under the tap. He
had an impression she was washing her hands of him. 'And
that's the easy part. The harder part is that people are dying
here. There's an open season on ANC people, you must just

read the papers.'

'I read the paper this morning,' Blade said. 'I guess I know what you mean.'

'Blade,' she said, 'I want you to know that I sincerely thought that we had something good going, but you must have heard that a thousand times already.'

'What do you want me to say?'

'That you'll try and save your life.' She gave him a chilling look and he imagined she saw him lying tortured, naked and dead on the page of a morning newspaper. 'We people who never went into exile – we had to deal with the shit in our neighbourhood. Teargas and guns and explosions and limbs and guts spattered all over the show. I am not a political person, I never was. But I have eyes that can see – and what I have seen is enough. I am one of those who believed that one day men like you are going to come with guns in hand and help free the country. All of us used to shout, *"Mayibuye!"* with our thumbs stuck out like this.' She made a fist which looked like a child's, and smiled at a grim memory. 'We loved then. We loved the sense of community, the togetherness. Nights blazed and introduced the horror in the morning, but still, we held on to one another, like a whole community of brothers and sisters.

'There was this time, Christmas 1989,' Lungi continued, 'and the children came and told us that Inkatha would be attacking. You see, at G and F and K and E Sections – the people knew that it was a no-go area for Inkatha. They had been beaten even when they came with the ZPs. So, we must have relaxed a bit. But now the children were telling us this story. And most of the men were at work or – as usual – in shebeens, getting drunk.' Wrinkling her nose, she pronounced the last phrase in English: *gettin' dronk.*

'We knew they would be coming in through *ezimpohlweni* – the hostels. Which meant they would have to cross the railway line between Thembalihle and KwaMashu stations. There was a possibility that they would railroad the residents at B Section, or even pick up some reinforcements at D or C.

'That was when the women, whose grapevine is more effective than all the telephone wires in the city, got together and marched. We walked from here to K and J and L and M, picking up anything that wore a skirt. Everybody. Beauty queens marched with shebeen queens and schoolgirls; teachers, off-duty nurses, domestic workers, people who would be doing night shift, *zonke zothayi, kwaba ududulayini, ngempela* – and we were singing, Blade. All these women were singing:

> *Wathint'abafazi*
> *Wathint'imbokodo*
> *Uzokufa!'*

and, as she sang, Lungi stamped her foot on the tiled floor, shimmying, doing the *indlikizane*. Blade, who knew the township mamas, imagined this cloud of angry womanhood. He smiled.

'It's no laughing matter!' Lungi snapped. 'At least, the Inkatha impi wasn't laughing.' But, despite herself, she began to giggle. 'Some of the mothers, scared of leaving their sons alone in the house, dressed them in women's clothes and forced them to join the march. And some transvestites, *ongqingili nezitabane*, came out, too, on this day of liberation and added colour to the procession.'

The march leaders called a halt at a spot along the main road running from the township gates to the end of D Section. There was a low bridge which was known as KwaVezunyawo, whose steps leading to the other side were usually covered with dried blood, piss and vomit. It was a notorious spot, hence its inelegant name which conjured images of people who had been robbed and dismembered. The women waited, singing their songs repeatedly; the impi came from the other side, also singing, jazzing themselves up for an orgy of mayhem. They saw the women. The hundreds of marchers sent an ear-splitting ululation, dancing and raising the dust. The police who stood watching – as was their fashion – from a safe distance diverted traffic, waving delivery vans back. 'The township goes crazy at the sight of a delivery van,' Lungi observed drily.

'The more daring of the women', she said, 'stepped forward and bared their breasts, singing and taunting the men, telling them that it was because they were not men that they spent all their time killing people. "Come on," they shouted, "come and get us and we'll show you your mamas!" The men shook their heads and got into a huddle. A helicopter hovered above this confrontation; later, after curses and promises of a bloody end to women's meddling, the men left with their tails – and a lot besides – between their legs, and the singing was considerably less heroic.'

'Was this reported in the papers?' Blade asked.

'Ja,' Lungi said. *'Ilanga Lase Natal* made it look like women were out of their minds, saying that people had been baring their breasts and all that. But some papers, such as the *New African* – which is not Gatsha's favourite reading material – reported with dignity. The editorial took issue with those who aren't committed to the peace process.'

Blade looked at the flies; they still moved slowly, inching up the lace. The sun which came in through the window to wash the aluminium sink; the hum and buzz of the township outside; the voices that entered in snatches: mothers yelling at the children and the children playing: all this became the sight and sound of home. He thought about the dead people, a drop in the ocean of corpses that had been piling up since the beginning of *udlame*, the troubles, in the country. While he was looking at Lungi as she made tea, feeling like telling her he didn't want any since he had a hangover but deciding to do the right thing, something in the way the sun caught the side of her face as she moved reminded him of his sister Nomusa. What had happened to her? How long was it now?

He had returned to KwaMashu after Groutville and searched the cemeteries for his sister's grave. What hurt to the quick was the revelation from the burial official that, even though there was a grave marked with her name, someone else, a fifteen-year-old girl, was buried there. This knowledge, that he could never really finish the process of mourning without seeing her grave, rocked him. He drank and brawled and played the saxophone with a group of musicians he had known before leaving the country. Blade knew, even in the deepest throes of inebriation, that all this was a futile attempt at forgetting the unforgettable; he was merely delaying that moment when the tears would flow like a river after heavy rains. When he played, then, he enveloped himself in a shroud where it was possible to remember without pain. The notes that poured out of the saxophone's brass bell were the unshed tears; they carried in them years of suppressed rage and longing.

He had been shocked, one day, as he walked down Albert Street, when he stumbled into Lungi. They had been at school together, oh, so many years ago. What amazed him was that, although the years had taken their toll, she was still Lungi. He had remembered some of the guilty moments when, as an acne-ridden adolescent, he and the other boys had used mirrors to try and look up women's skirts. Lungi had always been a mystery. When the boys indulged in communal masturbation, it was her image which caused him to groan and spill his seed in the urinal.

'I didn't know', she laughingly told him later when he revealed his earlier fantasies to her, 'that you had such a dirty mind – and fingers! And there we were, the girls, thinking you were such a nice boy!' Blade said: 'Nice boys are the worst when it comes to those things.'

She had accompanied him to the performances, more out of duty than anything else. Furthermore, it also meant she could keep an eye on him. It was in the way she held him that Blade knew how terrible the beast of loneliness was. He was lonely himself, and this clawed at him in the midnight hour, and caused him to sigh and moan. He felt guilty, when they were making love, when images of other women flashed before him like apparitions from a past that refused to be obliterated. Something in him said that this was wrong and indecent. Wrong because, here she was, Lungi, overflowing with an emotion she expressed as love, and he was incapable of reciprocating. Judging himself unselfish, he wrestled with the meaning of surrendering one's personality to another. What was love if there was no give and take? Women had this great capacity to give and receive nothing; and men the world over strutted on the sidewalks of time with their shoulders braced against the moment when they would be called to settle the account. Because, he knew, someday – a day that was soon a-coming – the women would rise up, much like the marchers of KwaMashu, and demand a better deal. What would happen then?

Even in the camps, he thought, the language that tried to decipher the hidden codes of gender failed. We spoke of building a new man – and this formulation came as easily as breathing – and we never saw the paradox, the immense irony in it. When women fighters such as Thandi Modise were praised, the comrades would say, She fought like a man. Blade would wonder, at moments when he could still think as alcohol burned down his throat, whether the new South Africa would usher in a different impulse; whether men and women would enjoy relationships on a common footing without something unnameable snarling in their midst. He knew that it would be hard, since, for him, whatever relationship he had with women was burdened by the baggage of tradition and custom.

His sister: she must have been a woman to those she interacted with. She must have loved and been loved in some panting instance of her life. He tried to imagine her with a lover, wondering whether she, too, had been capable of opening up like a flower and whisper the name of her heart. What had she thought about when she died? Had it been painful?

'You're crying again,' Lungi said. He knew that he had been doing a great deal of crying since the return from the cemetery. He had been woken up by his own choked sobs at night, and Lungi had cradled him, sometimes going as far as singing a lullaby, doing anything to connect him with a life he once knew so many decades ago.

Because, he felt, what else was left but tears? The township and its rhythms, the children who played and imitated adults at war: what was there for them except a legacy that was as obscene as an open grave? And the people themselves: every day they struggled against insurmountable odds, going into trains that shuddered with them daily to arenas of battle. In the factories, offices and the madams' kitchens, the people would encounter contempt as real and corrosive as desert storms. They would swallow insults from the children of the powerful, their eyes choosing not to see the faces of the parents congealed in distorting hatred. The mamas brought back fruits and vegetables from the markets and the fathers returned with more tales of woe. The evening meal would be a theatre of coded words and inexpressible gestures where the eyes of the children would be watched; because, no matter how irresponsible they might finally be judged, parents are uneasy with terror touching their children.

He remembered one of the first days back in KwaMashu when he drove with Lungi and her friend Juliet to Entuzuma, a sprawling expanse of township houses which stretched from the hills of KwaMashu to the edges of Inanda. On the way, they found twelve- and thirteen-year-olds filling a rut on the road with earth and stones. The kids stopped the car, and their leader, an unsmiling boy wearing a khaki felt hat, approached Blade's side.

'We have fixed the road for you,' he said, 'so that your cars can have a smooth ride. Now, *ngicela nisixhase.*'

'What does he mean, *sibaxhase*?'

'He means they want support for their effort,' Juliet said. She seemed uncomfortable with the kids. 'Just give him any coins you have.'

Blade took out a bunch of coins from his pocket and, without turning them, dropped them in the open hands of the boy. He was totally illiterate with the new coins of his country. He couldn't separate the new two-rand coin – called De Klerk – from the twenty-cent ones. What the hell. When they drove off to the salute of the kids, he asked: 'Is this happening a lot?'

'You mean kids acting like the Highwayman?' Juliet asked, relieved. 'All the time. At least these didn't threaten to smash the windows or burn the car. Kids have been known to force you out of the car and take it. And there's fuck-all you can do about it. This is the future of our country, Blade.'

'And the parents? What do they do?'

'Nothing. The parents themselves are in need of someone who can *xhasa* them.' It was as if Juliet was irritated by the question. 'This is our reality.'

It was this reality – the reality of all the blasphemed days – which forced Blade to think about the meaning of life. He could shed tears but what help was that? There were positions he had taken on violence; he would never again carry a weapon, or take a life. But, the images in the newspaper, the shells of men and women that had once supported life: what was to be done to stop all this? He felt the throbbing headache and knew that he was in for a bad day, and this thinking wasn't helping matters much. But he had to think.

When the fire blazed in the townships during the States of Emergency, people had debated about the use of necklaces on informers. He had been one of the people saying that this practice was wrong; it was barbaric and repellent. The standpoint of other comrades was that the necklace was a necessary method to discourage the informing that had led to so many deaths, that was causing the struggle to drag longer and longer. 'Look at it this way, *chumza*,' someone pointed out, 'if there were no informers, *izimpimpi*, we'd have long done one thing with the Boers.' But Blade was still convinced that, while it was true that one had to fight fire with fire, the necklace wouldn't bring the liberation day any closer. Killing informers just meant adopting the patterns that the revolution advocated against.

Then there was the time spent fighting Unita, something he could justify, the same way he could wiping out an enemy platoon. But that was different, he told himself. wasn't it? It was war. And now . . . ? These bodies that screamed for some explanation – was this not war? The government in South Africa armed with its state machinery: had it not effectively declared war against its black citizens? It didn't matter that, in the main, the people who did the dirty work were themselves black – they were conscripted troops, handmaidens. Even as he thought, something nagged him. He couldn't shake off the feeling that all this was somehow connected to Nomusa's death. His sister must have known something about these death squads, professionals who had the uncanny ability to target ANC people. In solving the mystery of her death, Blade knew, he would come closer to the bottom of these killings. Nothing was unconnected.

'What's happening tonight?' Lungi asked.

'We're still playing at the club.' Blade drank the tasteless tea and wondered whether the nausea would rise and he would have to get to the bathroom. 'After this,' he said, 'I'd like to take some time off.' He thought for a minute. 'How much preparation has been made for the conference? Is it still going to be held here in Durban?'

'It will be in Johannesburg,' Lungi corrected him. 'Branches are meeting and people are discussing papers.' She paused and listened to the sounds outside, like someone who had been interrupted while making an announcement. 'Frankly, I wonder how the two Natal delegations are going to manage, what with all this violence!'

Blade sincerely hoped that the ANC's first consultative conference would chart a path towards peace. He had heard that Oliver Tambo would be returning back home for the first time in three decades. He hoped that the Old Man, or Bones as he was affectionately called by his peers, would bring with him the magic which had kept the liberation movement together for all these years. Perhaps, after the conference, there would be serious programmes to try to limit the violence which had racked the country – especially Natal – from coast to coast.

The hunchbacked hills and valleys of the land, the rivers and the steady rock, the city and the countryside: all had been touched by the violence. It was there in the packed kombis and bakkies which transported passengers between the city and the township, people squashed into one small dream like so many sardines. It would happen – it had been predetermined by laws of trade and commerce that a taxi can only make money by making as many trips as possible – that a vehicle would veer off the road and crash into an embankment with its screaming cargo. Blood would flow on some of the best roads of the country, trickling into the culverts that had witnessed so many such scenes in silence. The birds that flew above would stop in mid-air and gaze with uncomprehending eyes at the ease with which people died. Or the trains thundering into ruined tracks, the steel and timber splintering together with the bones. The government of the day would declare itself innocent, blacks have this bad habit of dying in the most unexpected places.

But the violence that chilled the blood came from the people. They stopped funeral processions and hacked coffins and caused mourners to flee. It was so bad that in some rural areas it was impossible to bury people during the day. Or: the atonal account by a dry-eyed specialist in the necklace: We really didn't mean to kill him. It sort of . . . happened. You see, he was there, and we had roughed him up a bit, and he already had that expression on his face of someone who had accepted death. We slung the tyre round his neck and poured petrol all over it, inside. And, when he was handed the matchbox and the stick, we told him to light it. I stood there, singing, and I heard the match rasping against the striker. It was a strange sound, something that will live with me for ever. And then, just the whoosh! and green and red and blue flame enveloped him. I turned away when I heard the eyes popping.

There was the case of a comrade who died in an Inkatha stronghold. His parents were informed in no uncertain terms that his body was not to be buried in the region. The people, who could not call upon others to help, carted their unmourned relative to another town where he could be buried in peace. The price of peace was too high. Blade wondered whether the conference would organise for some of these relatives to attend. People needed to hear these testimonies from Hell. The question was: who would bear to hear such a tale?

For, Blade told himself, this country beats Beirut or Belfast by a long mile; the murders and rapes have earned preternaturally beautiful cities like Cape Town the label of the murder capital of the world. The crack wars raging in Harlem and Washington pale into insignificance in the face of an impi armed with traditional weapons which changes the history of a settlement and turns people's lives upside down. And the sun shines in the morning on those whose hands are filled with the blood of the innocent. White men go on making love to their wives and strike their children, and have their bacon and eggs and on Sundays go to the chapel and worship their Saviour, nothing in their eyes communicating what they have sanctioned. The wives in summer frocks and sun bonnets and sunglasses holding on to their charges who, born innocent in a guilty land, already know how to own and command, their eyes not reading the ghastly headlines about people who have been slaughtered on their behalf. The way meat-eaters are at peace with the world after a filling meal on lamb stew. And academics and intellectuals from the university supply statistics and monitor violence in a land where it is a crime to nurse the wounded or give succour to the bereaved. Their findings take them to the capitals of the world where slides are shown and films are made and books are written and reputations established. What madness is this? Have these people ever gone out to look at the sea and the rivers and the azure skies that hover above mountain ranges, stretching in summer as the breeze lets the cottony clouds ride like waves? or the trees, some with no name, and the herbs that breathe a pungent scent of healing and strength above the dark upturned earth which is supposed to support, to *xhasa*, all life? or the breathtaking viridian beauty of the Valley of a Thousand Hills? Do they not hear the songs of nature, the symphony of stone and sand and birds that sing even to the springbok in a trap?

But now we all smile, baring the teeth of ceremony. The exiles move from lands that become forgotten as time passes. The women ululate in a wedding or when someone gives birth, the cry no different from the keening wail at the graveside. The men jump into the nearest beerhall and drink and drown and rise no more. The young ones watch. They see their friends growing up in despair; the young woman with eyes as ageless as the sun knows her body is being watched by wolves. The wolves laugh and slink into corners and blow another blast of Durban Poison and a desperate drunk sings 'Swing low, sweet chariot', wishing for caring human hands to hold him and carry him home. But where is home? Tears sprang into his eyes again.

'Why did you come back, then,' Lungi asked, 'if this country gives you so much pain?'

'Why do people return?' Blade countered, knowing that the answer lay somewhere deep within himself. 'Mainly because exile is so intolerable, no matter what people say. And there is always that wish, when you are outside, to taste again the air of the country that brought you up. To find out if all the dreams you had, the images you conjured, are true. I know', he went on, shaking his head, 'that it sounds silly and coy. But for most musicians and writers, exile kills creativity. We moved along, allowing ourselves to be swept by a wave, having no control. Writers had to depend on street maps of their mother country. There was the miserable partying where we told each other how much we would make it in London, how South African creativity had also contributed to humanising the Brits. But the question we hardly asked ourselves was: Did the British public need us? We certainly needed them, no matter how we pretended otherwise. And – this was startling – we found out in the loneliness of our flats that we who had intended to change other societies had actually been changed by them. So, who won? I found out, for instance, that I liked my flat, the freedom of being alone on my own terms. I realised I hated any invasion of my space, which is a very British thing. I was every day sloughing off the skin of Africanness. But, on a spiritual level, Britain was beginning to make sounds with which I couldn't identify, and all the while I was outside myself watching me in this predicament. Life there was like looking into a mirror whose surface has dulled, leaving a blankness that was quite frightening. I saw myself spending another winter, bleak and grey, with everyone cursing that the sun sets at 4 p.m. And all of us, in the Underground, locked up like moles, all of us thinking of suicide. I was becoming quite self-destructive.'

'But', Lungi dug in, 'this country hasn't exactly been the elixir of life, has it? For you?'

'My reality has been fucked up for me,' Blade said. 'But still, there's something to claim here, which I couldn't find in Europe.' He tried to shape a coherent argument for being back in the country, and then it hit him like a bolt. 'The bones.'

'What?'

'The bones,' he repeated, gazing into the glass which had now darkened as a cloud passed. The mystified flies held on and then let go. The memory, triggered by something unknown, a quality full of changing and stilness, like a heartbeat, brought it all back. It had been hidden in some deep corner of his mind, waiting like an Easter chicken, to burst out into a new day. 'The bones have always been there, laughing at our stupidity.'

'Maybe', Lungi advised, 'you should take an aspirin and lie down.'

'Do you remember . . . ?' he started to say and then stopped himself. Of course she wouldn't. He was again confusing her with other women. He was suddenly impatient with her and wanted to get away. But, at the same time, he dreaded going out alone. The weight of the months spent in the country came and rested on his shoulders; the longing and the wish to comprehend the workings of the hearts of men and their gods became a living thing that sapped his energy. He was no different from a man with an *ilumbo*, a ravaging disease which confounds the best healers. Making a tremendous effort, he stood up and shuffled into the bathroom. His eyes accusing him in the unblinking glass, he held on to the bowl and threw up. The long process left him weaker than before, the sweat pouring out of him like a stream. When done, he rinsed his mouth and cleaned up, vomit reeking of bile, recycled malt and spirits. He felt empty, like a new vessel.

He woke up later when the Friday evening whispered itself into his dreams. They had been hard and unattainable, shadows that danced and reminded him again of the bones. Outside, the cars rolled on but now with a muted sureness, as if the dark were a cloud that cushioned everything. Feeling mellow and hungry and hard, he turned to Lungi, who lay awake in companionship of healing and solidarity, the way people lie next to their ailing compatriots. He wondered what she had made of his delirious babble, because he remembered the dreams that had roiled and unfolded themselves in front of him like pieces from a frustrating puzzle. The voices that had been in his head; the screams and irreverent laughter: but he could shrug off all this now. The time to wrestle with personal demons was past. He felt a great tenderness envelop him like a veil. Somewhere, in a state of sleepy wakefulness, he had cried when he couldn't find answers to his confusion. In the vignettes that translated themselves into images, he had experienced a great sadness when he found that he couldn't blow any more; the mouthpiece of his saxophone had crumbled like rotting sugar cane and the sound had been akin to a death rattle. It was with great relief, then, that he found himself in the land of the living. He recalled the bile that had touched his brain, the bitterness he had felt against the people of his country, how he had condemned them and cast them into the deepest darkness. He knew – waking up alive and whole and sane insinuated this – that no

45

matter how crazy things might be, life was still a gift. It was short and, hence, it had to be cherished.

The misguided sons and daughters of the masters of the land, he told himself, would one day wake up and their eyes would be opened and they would see that the promised land was more livable when shared among the people. Those who held on to national anthems and monuments and icons which excluded others, would know that a melody is enhanced by more people singing the same song. The worship of heroes and generals decorated in obscene wars of aggression was as obsolete as a pillory; men and women of the world had to move with the times and sing a song that would bind them and glorify their common humanity. And the children of the world would understand – this knowledge would be painful but necessary – that paradise is acquired at a price, and should never be forfeited, and that love is a bounty which nature bequeaths on the deserving.

Where there had been turmoil and turbulence, a calm reigned and Blade Zungu, musician and reluctant returnee, heard himself calling out her name. Then he stretched his hand and touched her on the hip, feeling the heaviness between his legs, something rising like a tide; and he caught the smell of the room, the perfume bottles arrayed on the dressing-table – and she murmured and edged closer and stuck her tongue in his ear. Then his fingers, working involuntarily, peeled off the thin blouse she had changed into, and he felt the satin skin beneath, warm and cool, the rising mound of her breasts, the nipples. He tasted them and rolled each one in his mouth, alternately, mischief guided by a need to discover and savour. The tight braids under his hand, her neck arched, the fingertips stroking the nape, a tender spot. Then the night darkened and the playing ended with the bodies wrestling on the sheets, time suspended, their breath making a statement that has eluded the wisest of men, the flesh speaking in tongues until the release – *yebo! yebo!* – and the savage tremors abated and the storm transcended itself into an indelible commemoration of tenderness, the final clenching.

A Gathering of Bald Men

Caleb Zungu was forty-three years old, married to Nothando
for thirteen years with two girl children, Busi and Khwezi, aged
eight and fourteen. He owned a house in Norwood, a car and
two dogs of dubious pedigree. He was an insurance salesman
for Allied Life, where he had worked for five years. He was
overdrawn at the bank and hoped for an act of God, perhaps
the death of a long-lost uncle who would leave him a handsome inheritance. Nothando had graduated from Kelly Girl to
a full-time employee in the Human Resources Department of
TransStar, a transport company. The girls were on school holidays, it being April, and the dogs, which he addressed in imperatives such as *'Voetsek!'* or 'Come here, boys,' depending on
his mood, were content with life.

On this late April Monday, Caleb woke up, took a shower,
brushed his teeth and dressed. He cut a dashing if formidable
figure in his navy-blue, pin-striped suit, a white shirt, a red tie
and black shoes. He drank his coffee quickly and went back to
the bathroom. Nothando almost dropped her coffee mug when
she heard a shriek coming from the bathroom. Thinking that
her husband might be suffering a stroke (as had afflicted two
male members in Caleb's family), she spilled her coffee in her
rush to see what was the matter.

She found Caleb, his head bent, gingerly feeling a bald spot
the size of an old one-rand coin which had, it seemed, developed overnight, on the crown of his head. Standing behind him
as he lamented his loss of hair before the unflattering mirror,
Nothando felt a pang of tenderness mixed with disappointment.
Why were men such babies? She managed to coax him out of

47

his dark mood, telling him that baldness was an attestation of virility, and that he looked very handsome and distinguished. Nothando resisted the temptation to kiss him on his pate, but firmly steered him to his car – a second-hand, shocking-pink Renault he had never got around to repainting – with encouraging words. Standing in the doorway and giving him the obligatory goodbye wave, which he didn't reciprocate, she knew that Caleb was deeply troubled; he hadn't even taken along his mobile phone.

While in the midst of preparing herself for work, her helper arrived and took over the necessary task of setting the kids on the straight and narrow. This might have seemed like heavy-handedness to the girls, especially Khwezi, who was spending too much time yakkity-yakking on the phone. This was a little worrying, especially since her daughter had taken to scribbling 'I ♥ JM' on her trainers and listening to Seal's crooning with a rapt expression on her face. Nothando wondered who the hell 'JM' was; probably one of those acne-ridden, foul-mouthed louts in oversized jackets, baggy pants and loose-laced, high-top trainers who slouched on street-corners, wolf-whistling at women. Although Nothando had ascended to suburban respectability, she still maintained contact with a few of the heavy brothers on the streets. If JM messed around with her daughter, she did not rule out calling in a friendly neighbourhood enforcer. It wouldn't do to let Caleb know of her anxiety; the way he felt, what with his loss of hair, they would have a homicide on their hands.

Nothando's lift came. Having negotiated the nerve-wracking Johannesburg morning traffic, she and Marcia, who drove a new Toyota Conquest, made it to the office on time. The Marketing Manager, Mr Peter Marshall, was forever bitching about punctuality. 'The RDP will go down the tubes', he was fond of repeating, like a preacher invoking holy writ, 'if you people keep this up.' *You people!* Nothando would think bitterly, these bastards never change, even if they pretend to be Jay Naidoo's lieutenants.

Nothando mulled over her husband's difficulty, knowing that some men had committed suicide at the loss of their hair. A man who does that wasn't fit to live anyway, she thought unkindly. Suicide, she believed, is the highest form of self-criticism. Caleb had told her of many people who had posthumously tried to gyp insurance companies by making their deaths look like murder or accidents. There was no bonus in killing oneself; in the credo of the Catholic church, you were even barred from entering that great festival in the sky. Nothando suddenly realised that she really didn't know whether Caleb was a suicidal type. The morning's outburst in the bathroom had shown another side to him. She'd be supremely pissed off if he took this way out.

She couldn't have known, however, that exactly at that moment, Caleb was in a boardroom where the Harvard-trained MD, Arnold Spicer, was reading everyone the Riot Act. The returns were low, much lower than had been forecast by the salesmen. When Sanders, a bright spark who specialised in retirement annuities, pointed out that there was a slump in the economy, Spicer retorted that he didn't give a rat's ass about the slump. 'The population is increasing daily,' he went on, 'and more and more people are growing older; they worry about death, so they need insurance. And you all sit here warming your backsides, telling me about the slump.' Well, thought Caleb, who was envious of the the fact that the MD had a full head of hair on his shoulders, it's good of him to say that; he doesn't have to pound pavements looking for clients. Caleb felt especially vulnerable, since his brief was to attract the black market. There was no percentage in this for the simple reason that the black business he 'solicited' seemed interested only in supporting the *black* market. Had he had it in him, Caleb would have informed Spicer that most black people also didn't give a rat's ass about insurance; some of those who did were slack in paying their premiums. When he called on policy-holders at weekends, he was certain that they had briefed their sons to tell him that, no, daddy's not home, he's gone to Thohoyandou. Caleb would know that he was being given the runaround, with the bastard who couldn't be bothered probably sleeping off a hangover.

Personally, Caleb had no time to cultivate a hangover, he was too busy. In one weekend alone, two dozen defaulters had gone to Thohoyandou, maybe there was an anti-insurance convention there. He had to devise another strategy to flush them out.

Caleb imagined himself a tolerant man. His job called for this. But one thing which was guaranteed to get his goat was people laughing at him. It wasn't so much that people didn't have money as that they were too lazy to reach into their jackets for the cheque book and sign on the dotted line. He remembered one office worker he had approached with the intention of selling him insurance. After the usual spiel to which the man listened attentively, Caleb had switched to the politically correct tack of how insurance helps the RDP. The man had laughed so much Caleb had feared he would rupture himself. 'You know what they call your RDP in the township?' he asked. 'Real Dummies Pay.' What was one going to make of these people? Small wonder he was losing his hair. For the first time after long months of abstinence, he felt like a drink.

As he drove along Empire Road, he cast around in his mind for famous men who were bald. There was Winston Churchill: 'It will be long, it will be hard, and there will be no withdrawal.' That was a classic piece, and Churchill was regarded as a sex symbol. Gandhi? Well, Gandhi was famous for other things, his glasses and the *dhoti*, he couldn't go that far; nor could he imagine South Africans following a leader who wore nappies. Bruce Willis? He was an actor, there was no guarantee that his scalp wasn't also acting bald. Was Hitler bald, or did he wear a hairpiece? What about Rajbansi whose wig had canted to the side when the *boers* manhandled him? Boy, that was sad – and on camera, too. If President Mandela were bald, maybe that would even the equation, lots of men like Caleb would walk with their heads held high. That De Klerk was no longer the top dog merely made matters worse. It made Caleb's baldness seem like a weakness.

He parked his car in Pretoria Street, in front of the Hillbrow meat market. Tossing a fifty-cent coin to one of the informal parking attendants lining the streets of the built-up areas of Johannesburg, he proceeded to the tavern at the corner. It was 11.30 in the morning; Caleb justified getting a drink this early by the peculiar nature of the day. Inside the bar, loud Zairean music issued from a stereo system. The interior lighting was rigged for a nightclub, strobe lights and weak bulbs dangling from the ceiling. This gave the bar a certain mysteriousness, a mixture of intimacy and menace. Dark men in the gloom drank their dark brews, speaking in low tones. The bar was a favourite haunt for drug dealers, illegal immigrants, people who operated on the peripheries of the law. Two women in loud dresses and high heels danced without spirit, their eyes luminous, like neon lights with some of the tubing missing. Caleb wondered if this establishment was insured against fire.

He chose a table that was farthest from the bar. The minute he was settled, a waiter ambled over and presented him with a menu. Caleb told him that he just wanted a drink. The waiter sullenly removed the menu and asked him what he wanted. Caleb settled for a beer, knowing that there was no trusting any other concoction. He recalled an English visitor who had ordered rum; on being supplied with a drink, the man took one sip and immediately passed out. Caleb listened to the throbbing bass and the wailing guitars accompanying an aggressive male voice. He was on his third beer, the dancing women beginning to have a certain raw sex appeal, when he considered suicide. He cried into his glass as he thought of Nothando and the girls. What would happen to them? He was overdrawn at the bank; even if his credit status were stable, he reasoned, the funeral parlour would no doubt make a big hole in his bank balance. Nothando would be left destitute, the kids – especially Khwezi, who was already a very combative teenager – would spit on his memory.

But the alternative was as bleak. He knew that losing his hair was a portent of a greater, more devastating loss. With his luck having run out at the same speed as defaulting clients, he could easily conjure up an image of himself, a few months from now, standing on a street corner carrying a placard with a message detailing his woes. He visualised himself totally bald, in tattered clothes, tapping on car windows, rattling a tin up some driver's nose. Maybe he should start now, learning the tricks of the begging trade. He thought of his children seeing him in that state, denying any knowledge of him in their shame, wishing him dead. Yes, he thought, death was better.

Already feeling relieved, as if a great decision had been made for him, Caleb placed a few rand notes on the table, stood up, collected his briefcase and buttoned up his jacket. It was then that a man entered and headed straight for Caleb's table. He was a gaunt white man about Caleb's age, with a weather-beaten, sallow face, his head as smooth as a billiard ball.

The khaki overcoat, a yellow sweat-shirt, ragged greyish trousers and Converse sneakers from which small brown toes peeped like mischievous children, gave him the look of an out-of-practice pickpocket. Rolled up under his arm was a piece of cardboard, greasy as if he had picked it up from the pavement. He gave off an odour of stale liquor, sweat and inner-city pollution. But there was something about the way he carried himself, his piercing slate-grey eyes, which distinguished him from the regular station crusty.

'Do I pass the inspection?' he challenged, drawing a chair and sitting down, looking up at Caleb. When the latter hesitated, debating whether to respond to the newcomer or just continue on his way as he'd intended, the man waved a proprietary arm over the chair Caleb had just vacated. 'Sit down, my friend. Sit down because you're going nowhere.'

Caleb had encountered people of questionable sanity before, and he knew how to make short shrift of them. But this stranger's confidence, the way he seemed to take over, calmed him down. He sat down. 'What's up?'

'You were thinking of killing yourself, weren't you?' the man asked, placing his cardboard scroll on the table. 'Been following you all the time. Said to myself: "That bloke's gonna do it."' He laughed; it was not a pleasant sound. 'You don't need to be a genius to know if a guy's gonna pop himself.' Then he turned and shouted at the barman who was eyeing them with amused contempt. '*Pilsner moja, bareki-sana.* That's Swahili for I want a beer, tot-quick!'

'Fuck off, Ranger,' the barman shouted back. 'I'm not giving you a glass of water until I see some money first.'

'O ye of little faith,' the man called Ranger lamented. 'Your obduracy will be your downfall yet, ye children of Mammon.

Who says I need to produce money? My friend here ...' and he tapped a long, bony forefinger against Caleb's shoulder, '... is on his way to committing suicide ...'

'Now, wait a minute ...,' Caleb started.

'... and I feel it's mighty unenterprising, certainly against economic growth, to die with a bundle of dough, don't you think?' Ranger was enjoying himself. 'I mean, inflation will have reduced those rands to scrip by the time you hit the Pearly Gates.' There was a general titter in the bar-room; even the dancers paused mid-step in their uninspired gyrations to appraise this fool who wanted to take his money to heaven. 'What's your name, friend?'

Caleb knew it was time he told Ranger where to get off. Pulling himself to his full height, he was about to let loose a salvo of imprecations when his gaze fell on the cardboard placard which had unfurled itself on the table. Written in uneven block letters, it read: TOM RANGER BLIND EX-SOLJER DONT NEED YOUR PITY BUT MONY WILL DO I DRINK AND SMOKE JUST LIKE YOU.

'Christ!' Caleb said; he was uncomfortable with any form of disability. He was suddenly at a loss for words. 'I'm sorry.'

'Yeah,' Ranger said carelessly, 'that's the way it is sometimes. Hope you don't mind the spelling, 'cause I dictated the damn thing to some cretin who can't spell to save his life.'

He turned his sightless eyes to Caleb. 'You haven't told me your name. Judging by your reluctance, it must be one of those well-kept state secrets.' He let this sink in, and then said:

'But first things first ... am I getting my drink or what?' As if on cue, the brooding waiter was suddenly hovering around with a tray; like a surly genie, Caleb thought.

'Give the man what he wants, and I'll have another beer,' he said to the waiter; turning to Ranger, he introduced himself. 'My name is Caleb Zungu.'

Ranger raised two fingers in the general direction of the waiter. 'Careful with the water.' He rested his arms on the table. 'And what do you do, Caleb Zungu?' Before Caleb could reply, he asked, 'You're some kinda salesman, aren't you?'

'*Ja*,' Caleb said. 'I sell insurance.' He paused. 'Does it show?'

'Man,' Ranger said, 'when I came in through that door, I got this vibe of sadness, you know what I mean, and I sensed this boyo out there in the corner, either drinking himself to a standstill or contemplating suicide. Or both. We blind *ous* can get so bloody annoying.' He gave a self-deprecating smile and spread his arms, his face lightening up the gloom. 'This fucking perception, man.'

Ranger was a hustler, Caleb judged, but he was of the honest type. The streets of Johannesburg teemed with people chasing the rand, some with ingenious schemes up their sleeves. The streets were also full of children who dared the unrelenting traffic, begging, making their plight known to all and sundry in the myriad tongues of the country. As a rule, Caleb never gave alms; the government had a responsibility for the destitute. Even if they didn't vote – and so much was done in their name – they were still the children of this Republic. Millions of rand were being squandered in buying military toys of destruction, in a country that claimed to have no external enemies; departments of social welfare enriched consultants, the same way that other government departments were throwing good money after bad in grandiose schemes and white elephants. As for big business, the directors were drawing salaries that boggled the imagination – their cars and their houses in Sandton could keep whole populations fed, clothed and sheltered for months on end. Furthermore, Caleb was damned if he knew now who was a genuinely deserving case. Most of the people on the pavements claimed they needed money for food; he was sure that, as soon as the coins added up, they would rush to the nearest bottle store. Once, in a rare moment of generosity, he gave money to a supposed beggar whom he later caught buying a copy of *Penthouse*. No sir, he wasn't a *moegoe* – a dummy. His mission on earth didn't include supporting someone's jerk-off habits. It wasn't lost on him that he was beginning to think like Spicer. Caleb had earned the money he didn't now have.

As Caleb and Ranger conversed about life and death while sipping their drinks – and as the latter made frequent tours to the toilet – more customers trickled into the bar, turning into a crowd. Men looked up and smiled or waved in recognition as

Ranger became considerably louder until Caleb told him to pipe down. He was entranced and repulsed in equal measure by this blind white man.

The blind eye of the seers. This thought came to Caleb, unprovoked, a comment on the situation in which he found himself. Or on the condition of business, where there was no vision. He had badgered the company to allow him to go to Pretoria and Cape Town where he was sure he would sell insurance to the batch of new parliamentarians. He had also been stopped from setting up a meeting with the RDP officers in Pretoria. Caleb had worked out a presentation he regarded as foolproof, where Allied Life would be seen to be an ally of the government's developmental programme. 'Johannesburg,' Spicer had said, 'or, more precisely, the township, is your bailiwick. Forget all that developmental stuff.' Other insurance companies had good working relations with government. Even formations such as Cosatu made it possible for insurance salespeople to have access to the workers. He, Caleb, was supposed to do business via the phone or on foot. He was in effect given a task he was not expected to accomplish.

But since Caleb was still determined to kill himself, Spicer and the insurance company became part of that other life, as remote as the stars, which would discontinue with his own exit. It suddenly felt good that he would not even miss it, there would be no room for such indulgence in the after-life. Caleb was a believer in life after death; he was convinced that ghosts walked in their midst, perhaps transmogrified into motes of dust such as these inside the bar which swirled desultorily in a single shaft of light. When a kid, his grandmother had impressed upon him the need to have respect not only for life but inanimate things as well.

Would sober up some of these drunks, Caleb thought, if some of the inanimate objects in the bar suddenly sprang into life.

'I don't get it,' Ranger drawled. 'You mean you want to kill yourself just because you're losing your hair?'

'Is there any other reason?' Caleb felt it would be futile to volunteer information about his status with the bank or frustrations at work. 'Isn't that enough?'

'I have helped many people commit suicide,' Ranger said. 'But it's been real desperate cases. Like this one guy who got impotent and his wife started playing around. Even if he could have regained his manhood, his marriage was gone, *kaput*. Because he would for ever be haunted by images of his wife swinging with another fellow, enjoying it – know what I mean?'

Caleb nodded. He was familiar with the humiliation facing a cuckold. There was a time when he suspected Nothando of seeing another man. It was then that he learnt of the destructive nature of jealousy. When she dressed and applied make-up, he concluded that she was tarting herself up for a tryst with her secret lover. Two of his best friends intervened and advised him that he was acting like an idiot. Nothando was a solid woman. This warning was timely, because Caleb had started following her, expecting to catch her *in flagrante delicto*.

Caleb knew he was by now quite sozzled when he started thinking in correspondence school Latin. His tongue felt as if it had swollen up in his mouth. Yet, he took another draught of his beer, convinced that it was better to die *non compos mentis*. He liked that phrase. Were it up to him, he would make his insurance pitch in Latin, see how Spicer liked that up his bloody white bailiwick.

'Do you want me to help you?' Ranger asked.

'Yes,' Caleb said. 'I just don't need no preambles. No last-minute sermons about the sanctity of life, or that my wife and kids will be unable to make ends meet. Don't give me that. I won't buy it.' A bad conscience nagged him, though. He knew that he had to devise a plan that would make his death look like an accident. The eyes of the children stared at him from the bottom of his beer tumbler.

'How do you wish to go? A bullet in the back of the head? Poison? A rope? Well, that's not really pleasant.' Ranger bent forward in the attitude of a conspirator, managing, however, to look like someone suppressing a belch. 'You know, my dad was a hangman. He's unemployed now there's this moratorium on the death penalty. But in his heyday, he was in great demand. He strung up a lot of fellows, even in neighbouring countries.' He nodded, agreeing with something that spoke deep, deep behind the sightless eyes. 'And did you know that when they hang you in Pretoria, it's not strangulation, as most people believe, but a broken neck, that actually kills you?'

Feeling a little sick, Caleb admitted that he hadn't been aware of that. He regarded his strange friend with renewed respect. 'Is that where you learnt this … helping people?' He realised the stupidity of his question. 'You couldn't have, though, being blind and all …'

'No,' Ranger said, his hand flitting across the face, shielding his eyes with splayed fingers. 'This is a recent thing, five years back. I was in the army where I was training some rookies in handling explosives, you know, and the damn thing just went *ka-boom!* and that was it, bye-bye eyes.'

Ranger then turned his eyes to Caleb as if he were seeing him. 'I was lucky I didn't lose my hearing, or my life.' He chuckled. 'My old man would have been mortified.' Then in a sing-song voice so low that Caleb had to lean forward, Ranger intoned something which sounded like a prayer:

No longer mourn for me when I am dead
Than you shall hear the surly sullen bell
Give warning to the world that I am fled
From this vile world, with vilest worms to dwell.

Then the music stopped and the clock somewhere inside the bar chimed the hour. As if this was a signal, Ranger got to his feet, rolled up his placard. 'Drink up, friend,' he said. 'Bill Shakespeare tells us it's time.'

'Was that Shakespeare you were quoting back there, then?' Caleb asked as they made their way out of the bar.

'*Ja*. I felt it would be a good epitaph for you.'

Caleb said nothing for a while, feeling the weight of Ranger's words. The man was a crank, no doubt, but he possessed a deep well of intelligence and experience on which he could draw at will. Caleb suspected that his own failure in life could be ascribed to his inexperience. If he had meant to continue living, he was certainly going to spice dinner-table conversations with some of these gems which tumbled so effortlessly out of Ranger's mouth.

It was a clear, bright April day when they went out, and the sun shimmered upon Caleb's eyes. It seemed as if the population of the city had trebled since he entered the tavern; young men dressed for winter lounged around doorways. The sex industry, since the ushering in of the new dispensation, was flourishing with hoardings tacked against walls advertising stylised sex paraphernalia. Market stalls weighted down by gigantic avocado pears, cabbage, tomato and an assortment of juicy fruit, replicated themselves on street-corners. Rising above the purr and roar of traffic was the strident whine of the butcher's electric saw. Women and girls sat on woven mats along the pavements, selling bolts of cloth, cosmetics, watches and tape cassettes. The heady Zairean rhumba rhythms Ranger and Caleb had endured in the bar now reverberated from speakers articulated to shop fronts, significantly heightening the temperature of this autumn afternoon. Here, on the pavement and on the road, people walked as if this were the first day of creation, some toddlers straying off to touch flowers, tweak the cheeks of dolls or feel the texture of calico prints; here, an entire lounge suite upholstered in carmine leather seemed naked on the open ground. An old man, like the victim of a recent eviction, sat in one of the arm-chairs reading the Bible, oblivious of the frenetic goings-on around him. This short walk to the car gave Caleb a strange thrill, the pastel colours of walls reflecting on the polished bodies of passing cars, and making a swift haze. He looked at all this energy, life in motion, stamping it in his memory as if with indelible ink.

As they neared the car, Caleb asked, 'What do you do, when you're not ...?' He fumbled for a word which would be less offensive than either 'begging' or 'hustling'.

'Ripping off you sighted buggers?' Ranger finished for him. 'Playing Scrabble. Had meant to patent blind players' variant of the game, but some eyeless smartass beat me to it.'

He smiled. 'My plan was for a multilingual game, and that means the value of the tiles would be different. I was already speaking to a Zulu teacher who wised me up to the preponderance of q's and z's in African languages. I'm still thinking of developing a slang, you know, *tsotsitaal* Scrabble.'

Caleb knew it would be useless to tell Ranger that *tsotsitaal* was something which developed each day. And that, like Arabic, it took on new forms from region to region. The irony of it all, that the township slang had actually increased in use in direct proportion to the heightening of repression, was not lost on him. But he had other matters with which to wrestle.

'This your car?' Ranger asked, exploring the contours of the vehicle. He yanked the door handle and when it didn't open, stretched out his hand. 'Gimme the *fokken* keys, Zungu.'

'What?'

'I said gimme the *fokken* keys, I'll drive.' There was a suggestion of great violence barely held in check in Ranger's tone. Caleb had an image of crazy, blind fury unleashing itself upon him. He surrendered the keys. Ranger got into the driver's seat and adjusted it.

He leant sideways to unlatch the door lock and let Caleb in. Instinctively, Caleb pulled the seat belt to strap himself in. 'No seat belts,' Ranger said. 'You want to die, don't you?' He turned his eyes in the passenger's direction. Then he inserted the key into the ignition, released the handbrake, and felt for the gears. '*Ja*,' Ranger said as he steered the car slowly out of the parking space onto the road, 'we're now in business.' Then Ranger stepped on the accelerator, sending the car shooting up the thoroughfare, scattering a group of Mozambicans like skittles. 'Used to drive in New York,' Ranger said as he gunned the car past the amber lights on the left into Abel Road, edging off a minibus.

The taxi hooted as it avoided Ranger, almost cannoning into a Clover Dairies delivery truck.

'Simple city to drive in, New York. Perfect for blind people like me, with all that Braille from the pot-holes.' He paused to stick his head out of the window and curse the taxi driver.

'What's the matter with you, man? You blind or something?'

While all this was taking place, Nothando was idly leafing through magazines such as *Cosmopolitan*, *Style* and *Drum*, pausing to scrutinise the advice columns. She read Tom Crabtree's contribution regarding male baldness. Quickly tossing the magazine onto the desk, she put on her jacket and picked up her handbag. Marcia was in the office kitchen, drinking her ump-teenth cup of coffee while holding forth about sugar daddies. Nothando caught her friend's attention, tapped her wrist to in-dicate that it was lunch time, and retreated into the lobby. Most of the typists, young women who worshipped at the shrine of the shopping-mall, had long broken off for lunch. Only a few stragglers who were victims of tyrannical superiors were still at it, tapping at their keyboards and brusquely responding to telephone inquiries.

Hell hath no fury like a woman done out of her lunch hour. Nothando remembered a story she had heard from one friend who was a returned exile. The secretarial staff at the ANC head-quarters in Lusaka was sent on a course where people learnt, among other things, telephone manners. The then-president Oliver Tambo called his office. 'ANC headquarters,' a smooth voice said, 'Dudu speaking, good morning, can I help you?' Tambo had to ask twice whether this was the ANC office, possi-bly wondering if his organisation hadn't been taken over by the Swedish embassy, before he was convinced that he was pho-ning the right place. Listening to the hum of computers and the constipated belch from the photocopier, Nothando marvelled at the amount of paper that got pushed every day in the office.

Accompanied by Marcia, she now showed her pass at the security gate and waited while Marcia opened her door. Nothando felt unaccountably tired; the strain of work combined with what had become the thankless task of raising two head-strong girls was beginning to tell.

Moreover, she had a feeling that Caleb was soon going to develop into a headache. Funny, she thought, how you marry someone and he looks like your dream man; then, *bang!* some-thing transforms him overnight into a pot-bellied, spindly leg-ged, old man whose bristles irritate you. Many of the women in the office were unashamed about the means they employed to offset suburban ennui. But she was past playing games. Nothando had once seriously considered an affair, but her in-ner self had cautioned against it; an affair was a headache. And then there was that eternal, fatal advocate of chastity, AIDS. In her line of work, she was duty-bound to counsel the staffers on the hazards of casual sex. Even though she had been thoroughly grounded in the workings of the dread disease, and how it could be contracted, she couldn't quite see herself telling a man to wear a condom. She had once tried one on herself and quickly discarded it. It had felt as if she were walking with a Checker's rustly carrier bag between her legs. So, no extra-marital *fickie-fickie*, as one of TransStar's more brazen Arabic customers would say.

Marcia interrupted her train of thought by suggesting that they skip the usual fare of spare ribs and chips and instead get some bagels with cream cheese from Feigel's kosher deli on Raleigh Street. The broad street of Yeoville was so full of people, some meandering aimlessly, that Nothando secretly yearned for the return of influx control. As she munched her bagel with the car rolling slowly down Hendon, she remembered the time when the sight of a uniformed cop meant that layabouts made themselves scarce. Now, she thought, *tsotsis* don't give a hoot; when they see a cop they try to sell him a stolen car radio. The spirit of new entrepreneurship, this morning's car attendant is tonight's mugger. Apartheid was bad, sure, but maybe it isn't right that people throw out the baby with the bath water. Some of the laws needed to remain, else how can a woman feel safe? People should get their priorities right, stop picking on poor Winnie and … Then she saw the car. There was no mistaking it was Caleb's pink jalopy. It streaked out of Abel into Harrow and almost flew into the brick wall behind which stood the Courtleigh luxury accommodation flats, narrowly missing a vendor who had been whistling as he stood on an unbroken line in the middle of the street. Marcia said, 'Isn't that …?'

'*Ja, uCaleb!*' Nothando screamed, reverting to Zulu, her primal comforter in times of crisis. '*Mlandele!*' She heard the screech of brakes and loud curses as drivers swerved to avoid the pink streak of madness bearing down on them. Marcia caught the light before it went red, turned the wheel hard and directed the Toyota down Harrow Road, herself missing a Volvo driven by Hasidic Jews. Three cars ahead, the Renault picked up speed, heading south. Nothando read the overhead blue-and-white sign, Doornfontein; where was Caleb going to, and at such speed? Marcia overtook two cars.

'Nothando looked out of the window, seeing the old Alhambra Theatre, a panel van reversing quickly into Bates Road. 'Don't worry,' Marcia said, beads of perspiration on her nose, 'I used to moonlight with Maxi Taxis ...' Then the skeletal railings on their left, beyond them the railway to Germiston, Brakpan, Benoni. Nothando looked at all these structures which were part of her city – strange now, much like the once-familiar car headed to hell – the mine dump, the old mine, the girders and cables bespeaking obsolete glories. Far ahead, above her husband's car, stood the rubber factory, Dunlop. She wondered why Americans chose to call condoms 'rubbers'. Caleb, you dumb son of a no-good bitch, she thought viciously, why are you doing this?

'He's trying to kill himself.'

This thought came to her just as she heard the sirens wailing behind. With it was a memory of Chris, an old childhood friend who had tried to kill himself. Having been jilted by his girlfriend, Chris announced to all and sundry that he was serious about suicide. Nothando and a group of friends – and Chris's reason for wanting to leave this cruel world – followed him unobserved as he sought a tree in Mofolo Park. They had never seen a person actually dying, this was going to be a golden opportunity. They watched him installing breeze blocks at the foot of the tree, loop the rope over the branch and secure the noose around his neck. But the tree was a sapling; it sagged with Chris, making Nothando think of one of those ineffectual snares township boys set for birds. Having failed, Chris trekked to the railway line near Orlando Station. He stretched himself across the tracks and waited for the train. The sun was hot, which meant that the steel tracks must have been blistering. Chris left the rail tracks to look for pieces of corrugated paper in the bushes. While he was reaping his strange harvest, a train rolled past. He went back to the rails and made a bed for himself. Nothando and her friends crouched in the tall grass, also waiting for the train. What came was not the train but a platoon of railway workers in their ochre overalls, each with the SAR&H logo on the breast pocket. They carried signs which Chris would have gratefully added to his bedding. The South African Railways and Harbours Union had called a strike earlier in the week; hence the scarcity of trains. The singing and toyi-toyiing railway workers made a sound not unlike the Kiwis' rugby *haka* when they saw Chris. Since being torn limb by limb was not part of his suicide repertoire, he got up and dashed into the bush, over the fence and onto steady township ground.

Nothando heard a loud crash as the pink Renault slewed off the highway into Rissik Street.

The sirens got louder; the vehicles to their left skidded and tortured brakes screeched as each driver strove to avoid being embroiled in a pile-up. Nothando couldn't remember when or how she had got out of the Toyota, but she found herself running towards Caleb's ruined car which had hit the railings and edged a quarter-way into space. Mangled steel and chrome, spinning wheels, scorpion-like breakdown trucks, flashing lights and the incessant scream of the siren – all these sights and sounds blended in Nothando's mind, releasing an impulse that had been struggling for expression in her chest.

She screamed: *'Caaaaaaaaleb!'*

This cry, coming from lungs which had been trained in church choirs, vigils and admonishment of rebellious children, rang above the roar of traffic, almost shattered the eardrums of nearby police officers and onlookers, and caused a flock of pigeons to start in mid-air and soar into the sheltering sky. It was heard in the offices of the car dealers along Eloff and Albert streets. Commuters coming out of Faraday Station stopped in mid-stride, pricked up their ears and rushed to the source of the scream. In an interview with the *Sowetan* later that afternoon, the chef, who had been sweating in the kitchen, abandoned his fried chicken at Chicken Licken because, for him, what he had heard was a trumpet heralding Judgment Day.

A burly policeman, Warrant Officer van Vuuren stopped his squad car and rushed into the mêlée. He shoved aside the curious onlookers until he got to the crashed car. Working with the breakdown attendants, he prised the doors open, dragged the two men out and laid them on the road. Nothando, breathless, rushed to Caleb's side, swabbing the blood off his brow with her jacket. Moaning his name repeatedly, she gazed upon his face, noticing as if for the first time that he had an old, cuticle-shaped scar above the left eyebrow. The realisation that she had missed this little detail brought about a gush of emotions she had never suspected she possessed. Nothando knew then that she loved Caleb, this fool, her fallen hero, who now lay like a log, breathing the foul smell of unwashed socks and tar. When he opened his eyes and smiled, Nothando almost wept with relief. Then her eyes were blinded by rage. She pulled him up until he was wobbling on unsteady feet. Pushing him against the car, she started pummelling him with her fists, shrieking, 'You bastardyoubastardyoubastard ...' until, spent, she collapsed against him. Van Vuuren, who obviously hadn't read Commissioner George Fivaz's latest tract on community policing, was busy slapping a groggy Ranger.

'*You fokken blerry mampara,*' Van Vuuren hissed, 'how many times have I told you to steer off trouble? You know that you're giving us *wit mense* a bad name?'

'Officer,' Caleb said, extricating himself from Nothando's arms, 'you can't do that to Ranger. He was trying to help me.'

Van Vuuren turned round and studied Caleb. 'You stupid idiot,' he said, 'you must count yourself lucky that he didn't kill you. This man', he continued, pulling Ranger by one ear, 'has been a *blerry* headache for us since leaving Sterkfontein.'

'No matter,' Caleb persisted. 'The man is blind, after all ...'

'Blind?' Van Vuuren laughed. 'Is that the latest trick now?' He turned to Ranger.

'Tell me you're blind, you son-of-a-bitch, and I'll personally *moer* your eyes out.'

'*Ag,*' Ranger said conversationally, 'be reasonable, *Kolonel.*' He shrugged. 'A *mens* has got to live, *mos.*'

The crowd which had collected petered out. An ambulance came and the two men were installed inside. Nothando climbed in and sat beside her stunned husband. Caleb still couldn't believe that Ranger was not blind. He wanted to dive across and beat him up, but he was feeling too weak. Even thinking about what he and Ranger had got up to was a strain.

A month later, Caleb resigned from his job at Allied Life and set up an organisation called Progressive Hairlessness Educational Workshop. Headquartered at a small office overlooking the new Constitutional Court in Braamfontein, PHEW, as it was popularly known, started off badly, with the media dismissing it as a monumental hoax. But they hadn't bargained for Caleb's tenacity. Working day and night, he canvassed his erstwhile insurance clients (and people didn't dodge him now that he was no longer a threat) and importuned bald celebrities in the Gauteng region to endorse PHEW. Ranger emerged from his adventures to lend a hand. The two men inserted advertisements in the papers, seized every opportunity to speak for the hairless on the radio. Using his insurance connections, Caleb patented a logo, an egg with a confident smile above and below, on which were arranged 'PHEW' and 'pride of the hairless' in lower-case red letters.

Letters from interested correspondents flooded the office. A controversy broke out (by then Caleb had shaved off all his hair) whether people with receding hairlines could take up membership in PHEW. Some prankster, no doubt an infiltrator, boasted on Radio 702 that he had a database of top leaders in industry and government who wore wigs. *Is baldness a private matter?* read a headline in the *Star* of the following day, responding to the idea of outing closet baldies. By now subscriptions were pouring in. Nothando's services were enlisted to deal with the increasing volume of work. After appearing in Dali Tambo's 'People of the South', Caleb and Ranger were invited on a nationwide speaking tour. A car company in Uitenhage purchased a franchise to market its latest model exhibiting the PHEW logo minus the lettering. Caleb, Ranger and Nothando registered PHEW as a listed company on the Johannesburg Stock Exchange.

Caleb Zungu was forty-five years old, married to Nothando for fifteen years with two girl children, Busi and Khwezi, aged ten and sixteen respectively. He owned a house in Norwood, two cars and two dogs of dubious pedigree. He was the chief executive officer of PHEW Enterprises. Nothando and Ranger were junior partners in the company. JM, who exhibited keen business acumen, was a favoured future son-in-law. His ready acceptance into the Zungu family was due to his premature loss of hair.

And the two dogs were called by their real names. Baldy and Beauty.

The Naked Song

On the day the Stock Exchange dropped a couple of points following the announcement of Nelson Mandela's confinement to
hospital for a prostate operation, a somewhat depressed Leonard
Gama sat in his office, watching traffic rolling by on a restless
street. Elevated above street level stretched a freshly mown
playing-field so green it could have come out of the pages of
a children's picture book. A gaggle of black and white boys in
grey trousers and white shirts and loosened ties passed a football around, dribbling and executing jubilant jigs.

Gama cast around in his head whether to read the morning
papers or intimidate the secretary into making him a cup of tea.
Magriet, a throwback to the good old days when blacks didn't
give orders, was for ever busy faxing her curriculum vitae to
companies and organisations which still pandered to nostalgia.
One evening, finding the gents' toilet inaccessible, Gama took a
chance and emptied his bladder in the ladies' where he gazed
with wry amusement at the legend scribbled with a koki pen
on the whitewashed wall: *Affirmative action is sommer 'n klomp
kak!* Gama considered himself lucky in not having struggled to
find a job. It could have been due to the shortage of black psy-
chologists; most companies snapped up the few there were and
exhibited them like hunting trophies in board meetings. He was
employed by the Sandor Centre, a group of consulting psycholo-
gists who specialised in psychotherapy, assessment and media-
tion. This was where Gama had to make hard-nosed decisions
regarding a rumour that there was a sympathetic black man
who dispensed free advice, leading to all sorts of people beating a path to his door. Before starting a consultation, Gama in-

formed the client that time was money. It wasn't always easy.

Returning to his homeland after two decades of exile had sensitised him to the difficult path his fellow citizens trudged every day. The government ministries and departments were usually housed in the same buildings or offices of the repudiated past. The personnel at the gates leading to the corridors of power remained as formidable as ever. Men as tall as cedars – and as wide – with moustaches resembling municipality brooms, towered above one and extended a hand the size of a graveyard shovel to accept one's written memo to see the Minister; the memo, as if frightened to death, shrinking in size to a postage stamp. Some of the ministers looked small and lost in chambers roomy enough to fly a small airplane.

Gama stopped and pondered, knowing that he was falling into the trap of cynicism; it was easy to cast stones at the fragile glass of the new democracy. But it still rankled that he was increasingly having to deal with instances of inefficiency which could hardly be attributed to the legacy of apartheid. He handled many cases which needed co-operation and support from government departments; he wasn't making any money. His other partners who acted as stewards to an endless stream of white neuroses made a killing. Most of Gama's clients were – for the mere reason that they had been cast so low as to need someone to advise them – not in an admirable income bracket. Furthermore, paying for advice was not at the top of most black people's agendas; hell, it would be like paying for an uncle's beneficence. The majority of defaulters were former exiles who had missed the vehicle which had catapulted their more fortunate brethren to lofty heights.

Sounds of a scuffle in the reception area interrupted his train of thought. Magriet, blonde tresses swishing threateningly, stormed into Gama's office. Her blazing eyes were an indication of her combative mood; at the same time she seemed to be struggling with her own personal demons.

'What's the matter, Magriet?' he asked distractedly, knowing that he was beyond surprise. The surprise would have been a whole day spent without a surprise; that came with the territory.

'These people,' Magriet said, half her visible figure shoving off someone unseen behind her, blocking their entry. 'They just barge in here without any appointment. What kind of business do they think we're running here – a blerry shebeen in a *skomplaas*?' As if on cue, the skirt of a serge greatcoat flapped into view, followed by a trousered leg, until a small, wizened man stood in the doorway. He grunted a greeting and rubbed his nose with the back of his fist. Magriet, her worst fears confirmed, rolled her eyes and, her frame rigid with indignation, stormed out of the office, leaving behind a lingering fragrance of wild flowers. The visitor was of indeterminate age with a dome-shaped head of uncombed hair peppered with grey. The eyes were quick, alert, at the same time maintaining that distant, downcast attitude of servility which most black people have honed to a fine art as a defence against white authority. Gama knew that most black people had been so beaten that they would tend to be tentative to other blacks who represented power. This knowledge that he could fill his countrymen with fear and trembling, did nothing to lift his spirits. Under the greatcoat, the old man wore a threadbare navy-blue suit, a grey shirt held at the collar by a red tie which brought to mind the tongue of a strangled bull. Magriet's fragrance was overpowered by a feral odour people would associate with the grave.

'*Siyabonana, Ndodana,*' the man greeted again.

'*Yebo, Baba,*' Gama said and pointed at a chair. 'Please take a seat.' He thought of offering to take the man's coat – the weatherman had forecast a sizzling day – but decided against it: he didn't want to leave this early caller bereft of what could well be his security blanket. 'What brings you here?'

'My name is Nkosi, Mr Gama,' Nkosi said after installing himself in one of the uncomfortable chairs. 'And this matter is not about me, really, although it concerns us all.'

Gama, elbows on the desk with his fingertips meeting to form a pyramid, nodded understandingly. Outside, the sound of traffic commingled with the gritty staccato bursts of a pneumatic drill. Loosely, he remembered an old friend who, after taking a couple of long drags from his *zoll* of Durban Poison, made this observation: 'You know, *Chumza*? Work *is* noise!' Gama smiled, remembering the sickly-sweet fumes of the prize weed. 'Who is it all about, then?'

'My son, Richard,' Nkosi replied and, in the same breath, bellowed, *'Richard!'* Gama was so surprised he started out of his chair, ears ringing. He had a distinct impression that the hum of the air-conditioning had stopped, as if its heartbeat had been disturbed. Gama wondered what Magriet was making of all this.

Richard, in his early forties, emerged. He was taller, stockier and infinitely sadder than his father. Dressed in a windbreaker over a yellow T-shirt, denim jeans and trainers, he might have been of a different breed, but he was definitely of the same seed. It was in Richard's eyes that Gama saw something which connected them both to a remote past. What was it?

Then it hit him. *Richard*! Of course, this was Richard, once a wiry devil who caused women to scream when he blew his tenor sax with the Amandla Cultural Ensemble in Angola. And that was, oh, how many years ago?

Gama went round his desk and strode to Richard. 'Hey, *camarada*,' he said, 'what are you doing here?' Praying for mutual recognition, he made to embrace Richard. But Richard took a step back and something harsh and disjointed came out of his lips. Gama looked past Richard's shoulder to see Magriet wearing a look with which parents favour a loved but headstrong child. She shook her head sadly.

'He can't talk, Len,' she said.

'What do you mean he can't talk?, Gama asked, feeling stupid.

'Just that.' The revelation of Richard's disability had softened something in her hard interior. This was one of Magriet's character traits which never failed to intrigue Gama; she could switch from being a witch possessing the sensitivity of a Parktown prawn to a candidate in the Mother Teresa school of piety. 'Must be mute hysteria,' Magriet put in. 'You know how that is.'

Gama, mentally riffling through the pages of psychology textbooks for case studies, turned to the old man. 'How long has this been going on, Baba?' The subject of the inquiry, Richard, perched himself on the corner of the chair, his whole pose indicating a readiness to flee.

'He was fine when he came back,' Nkosi began. He turned to his son and gingerly placed a hand on his shoulder, the touch gentle, as if he feared the possibility of a further wounding. 'You were all right, were you not, Richard? When you returned … from exile?'

Richard nodded and rubbed the bristle along his jawline. He seemed to shrink further within the windbreaker, much like a slug retracting into its shell after contact with salt. It occurred to Gama that, even if this young man with a ruined mind might be an issue of his father's loins, it would take volumes for the old man to start comprehending what Richard had gone through. Because, Gama knew, there was no such thing as returning from exile. Exile was not so much a geographic dislocation as a state of mind, something that consumed and branded and left one marked for life. Many, like animals whose limbs were left in a snare, walked through life crippled, their minds locked on that fateful moment of rupture.

Nkosi looked up at Gama. 'I don't know what happened.' He turned in his chair to gaze at Magriet, then back to Gama. 'It has something to do with a woman he met some time back.'

'My!' Magriet said. Shaking her head, she disappeared to tend to her secretarial duties at the front desk. Despite his irritation with her, Gama felt that he needed her support because this was promising to be a long day indeed.

'You can still write, Richard?' he asked.

Richard nodded. Gama pushed aside the papers on his desk. He retrieved a lined executive desk pad and placed it on the mahogany surface. Pushing forward a cracked earthenware jug containing an assortment of pens, he steered Richard to seat himself at the desk. 'Since we can't conduct this orally,' he said, remembering the time he wrote his own biography at the behest of the Recording Section of ANC Security in Angola, 'we'll just have to make do with the written word.'

He wished to sit down and tell Richard of his own bewilderment when he wrote his biography in Angola. The effort of trying to remember each detail of his past life. The fact that the Security comrades had the power to dismiss certain passages on paper as arrant nonsense. In a word, the powerlessness he experienced in recounting his life to strangers. Richard shot him a quick look. What was behind it? Recognition of a past kinship? Bewilderment? Gama couldn't tell. Richard then flipped the pad open, chose a pen and started writing. Gama went to the reception area, picked up the phone and ordered rolls and sandwiches, tea and coffee from the deli downstairs. Magriet put in for biscuits and cans of her favourite fizz. Obliquely, Gama recalled a television show where the black American nationalist, Stokely Carmichael, was being quizzed about his sartorial elegance. 'Mr Carmichael,' the unctuous interviewer, going for the jugular, asked, 'how do you reconcile your Brooks Bros suit, your silk rep tie and Florsheims that must have cost a pretty penny with your verbal fusillades against, ah, American consumerism?' 'Well,' Stokely replied, not missing a beat, 'you've got to eat while you suffer.'

Richard and his father ate while they suffered; in the meantime Gama mulled over Richard's problem. In his line of work, he had dealt with numerous post-traumatic stress disorder cases. While these differed in degree and range of severity – some being referred to other institutions – the task had been made somewhat clearer and more manageable by the possibility of dialogue between therapist and patient. With Richard, Gama could not have the benefit of the sufferer's nuance, inflection or cadence of speech, nor could he seize on nonverbal clues suggested by a telltale quirk or mirrored through eyes, facial expression or body language.

But if he didn't meet this challenge, he asked himself, who would? For multitudes, the return to the mother country after years outside was as bewildering as the first experience of exile. Although quite a few had been in contact with their countrymen and women – and knew of the changes that were taking place every day – something about the actual experience of walking on the sidewalks still stained with the blood of innocent children, seeing the grim stone edifices which had financed the might that led to their flight – the unchangeable nature of a myriad of institutions – left a bitter taste in their mouths. Many, then, had evolved stratagems to redefine themselves and recreate a piece of their country in foreign lands. They played music and reminisced over moments whose glorious nature was limned by longing. To fight boredom and despair, some of the exiles sought succour in the bottle and the weed. Quite a few found salve in the arms of strangers and thus staved off the hungry beast of loneliness. Legions found that the beast existed somewhere inside themselves and could not be appeased.

It was in the eyes of their children that Gama saw how the flight from oppression to the journey back had taken its toll. Because the young would always be looking for the promised land, and that land resided in the well-being of the parents. The children were quick to learn that what they had been promised as they were readied for the homeward journey was long in coming, and the edginess of the elders would deepen their bewilderment. Those weaned on the culture of video arcades and pool halls and easy access to shopping malls would balk at having their movements restrained.

Gama's eyes were drawn to the playing-field; a ball arced high above the heads of the boys, its momentary after-image seeming like a parabola against the deep green of the trees, and bounced soundlessly on the turf. Even from the distance of his window, he could see the intentness written on the players' faces, these children, a metaphor for the glory that was yet to see the light of day. For a long while, the phrase *levelling the playing-fields* had been so kneaded into the everyday language of the country that sharp township suitors were wont to employ it in their chatting-up repertoire: 'Hey, sister, I wouldn't mind levelling *your* playing-field.' The schoolboys, however, were concerned with neither politics nor sexual advances. Now they were playing exhibition soccer, passing the ball to one another with dazzling accuracy. Beyond them the trees seemed to groan under the midday haze which was as much a character of the city as was white to rice. On the pavilion sat a scattering of kibitzing schoolgirls, in shorts and tunics, their white T-shirts catching the sun, defining a range of the howlers' colours that spoke so eloquently of voyages, occupations and resistance. The Rainbow Nation, Archbishop Tutu had christened the children of the new South Africa. Gama wondered absently if these happy players and their reluctant supporters would ever find the pot of gold.

Of the many people who had come to the Centre on the second floor of the building, a few had left their memories clinging to the walls like wisps of smoke. There was Abner, who had been pursued by memories of storms. He told Gama that he was a rational man, but he was convinced – he saw it all – that the path to his house was lined with tombstones. He later took his life. There was Trevor, who had an obsession with doing everything right. He had stopped smoking and was by then a moderate drinker. Each time he went into his room he was convinced that someone had altered the arrangement of the furniture. This sense of displacement led to his spending long nights outside his house, staking out his domicile the way detectives keep watch over a dwelling in a contested divorce case. He would sleep in his bed and dream that someone who had taken over his body was also sleeping in a room which was a replica of his own, and was merely biding his time, waiting for the moment Trevor went into a deep sleep so that he could make the switch. At the end of the sessions, Gama had to refer him to the local School of Psychiatry. By then Trevor was absolutely sure that his room, the house and even the streets had been tampered with by someone, in his words, who wanted to fuck with his mind. There was, ah, there were so many. But this … Richard …

Old man Nkosi finished his sandwich and gulped down his tea. Pulling Gama aside, he confided that he had taken Richard to the *inyanga* in one of the hostels of Soweto. For a week Richard had been manacled to an iron-frame bed. The *inyanga* routinely pricked him with a porcupine quill. This was supposed to expel the evil spirit that had taken over his body. He had been to the spiritualists, who had prayed for the young man, laying hands on him, engaging in rites and rituals to exorcise the demons. Because, in the understanding of the traditional healers, the young man was possessed. All these attempts at healing failed. And vast sums of money were spent in the process. 'Richard trusts you,' Nkosi said. 'You *must* help him.'

When he left the office for the bank and some personal

errands in the city, Richard was still writing. Gama had fought the impulse to peer over the hunched shoulders for a glimpse of what must have been the most important – and painful – confession. He knew that this was Richard's private moment, even though his testimony would later be out there for Gama to read. Because, he knew, to strip oneself naked in front of others was the greatest expression of trust – and trust could not exist separately from love. When he came back, it was after two o'clock. Magriet had left for the gym. He wondered what she wanted there, really, seeing that she had the tight, trim figure scores of women immolated themselves to attain. Thinking about her, Gama experienced a hot flash of lust; but he was in the middle of a messy divorce and couldn't afford to complicate his life further . Moreover, he belonged to the school which believed that, in the words of a street poet, an African woman must cast a wide shadow.

Richard and his father had also left after rinsing the cups and consigning the remnants of their meal into a waste-basket. On the desk lay a brown manila envelope with the legend, *To Mr Gama, from Comrade Richard*, in a neat, sloping handwriting. The titles bespoke the existence of a gulf which needed breaching. Gama opened the envelope and scanned the pages, wondering whether the loss of speech also meant that Richard couldn't play music any longer. Was there any connection? Should there be a connection? Activating the answering machine, Gama chose a comfortable position and began to read.

Richard's story was at first typical. He was one of the thousands of young people who left South Africa after the slaughter of schoolchildren in Soweto and elsewhere in June 1976. He wrote like the musician he was, bringing out sight and sound in detail. His account was here and there inflected with humour, such as when he and three others crossed the Pitsane-Molapo river into Botswana. The exultation when their feet touched a piece of independent Africa. Then they saw a huge python coiled in a bundle across the path. One of the kids, who had never seen a live snake in his life, screamed, *'Voetsek! Voetsek!'*, shooing the snake away as he would a township mongrel. Richard remembered that, before slithering into the bush, the snake shook its head as if saying, 'Now I've seen everything.'

If Johannesburg had been exciting and dangerous, Gaborone proved one long session of waiting. The sun beat down with a ferocious intensity, the monotonous chirping of the cicadas and the schoolchildren singing in different sharps and flats caused everything to seem as desolate as a desert. The Batswana treated the refugees with a mixture of kindness and benign contempt. In all this, Richard practised his scores and sat in with a couple of bands.

Those refugees who had not cast in their lot with the Movement milled about the President Hotel from morning to nightfall. One student from Maru a Pula, when asked what she would like to be when she finished school, said that she would like to be a refugee, who would sit and drink at the President, speak English the whole day and at the end of the month get thirty *pula*. This was the monthly stipend refugees received from the United Nations via the Botswana Christian Council.

A new wave of exiles came in, artists, musicians, writers. In 1977 the University of Botswana became so pivotal in cultural activity that the country sat up and took notice. Richard joined forces with trombonist Jonas Gwangwa, freshly arrived from the United States, who was putting together a contingent for FESTAC, the Festival of African and Black Arts and Culture, which was to be showcased in Nigeria. It was also a period of heightened South African Security Police activity. Richard remembered standing in an immigration queue at the airport as the group of musicians and poets were on their way to Lusaka. Craig Williamson, corpulent, smug as a bedbug which battened on blood, was behind him, making small talk, a UN passport in his hand. He was to be central in the June 1985 raid on Gaborone when thirteen ANC cadres were massacred. Among them were Thami Mnyele, an artist of consummate skill, and Joe and Lindi Phahle who had been towers of strength, giving sustenance to the artistic community in many ways. 'White South Africans', Richard wrote, 'must not forget what has been done in their name.' Gama had himself seen how, in the name of reconciliation, there was a tendency in many convocations of the good and the great to inculcate a state of national amnesia. The past, which had dripped with blood and venom as mango dripped with juice, remained unacknowledged. The silence, then, was filled with the howling of those thousands who had been wronged, who had stood at gravesides watching the earth swallow their loved ones. For these, and many more, what was not forgotten could not be forgiven. What became a piquant flavouring of this strange fruit was that many people sincerely believed that they had murdered and raped for the sake of their children. These children, then, whose collective brow was stamped with the blood of guilt, roamed, looking for comfort in arms which could bear to embrace them; this, in a world that forgot nothing.

Lagos proved an eye-opener for Richard. Here thousands of artists, united by how thoroughly the white world held them in contempt, performed and exhibited their craft. There were fire-eaters from Surinam, dancers from Harlem; the colloquia were dominated by the expulsion of Abdias do Nascimento, who had incurred the wrath of Nigerian hosts by suggesting that racism was alive and well in Brazil. Stevie Wonder performed on the same bill with Miriam Makeba at the Tafawa Balewa Square. It was on the obelisk fronting the National Theatre, all countries represented by their flags, that Richard realised that he actually had no country.

The high point of the festival was when the then ANC President Oliver Tambo and Thabo Mbeki, then ANC Chief Representative in Nigeria, visited the contingent at the FESTAC village. Tambo, who seemed preoccupied with grave matters, gave the contingent encouragement, stressing that culture played an important part in the struggle. Some of the men and women asked questions, but Richard sat, awed by the leaders' presence. That night, the South African musicians blew up a storm.

When his mother died and he could not go home to bury her, Richard grieved alone. He knew that she had loved him and now he wanted to tell her how much he loved her, too. He wanted to prove to her that he would make something of himself yet, and that he was not as full of the devil as she had thought. Her death brought to him the knowledge that he had been playing for her, that, even if the whole world would be struck deaf and dumb, she would be there to hear him. Now that she was gone, everything seemed meaningless. When playing music started losing its earlier appeal, he hit the bottle. In many instances he found himself in brawls or waking up beside a nameless stranger, his nostrils assailed by the stink of stale alcohol, bodily funk and joyless sex. A long moment of self-disgust would follow; cobwebs would clear somewhat after the first draught of Castle Lager, then the cycle would start all over again.

It was on such a morning when his mouth felt as if it housed the nest of a weaver bird when there was a knock on his door. Who could this be? he wondered. Collecting himself, he padded barefoot across the cement floor and opened the door. Two men, Keith and Scara, stood on the threshold. They looked so fresh and smelt so strongly of Lifebuoy soap that Richard felt his gorge rise. After a greeting, he reluctantly let them in. They didn't waste time telling him the reason for their visit. 'Pack your things,' Keith said. 'There's a car waiting for you, you're going.'

'Where? What?' Richard asked.

'You said you wanted to be a soldier, didn't you?' Scara asked. 'People are waiting for you. Snap it up.' He wrinkled his nostrils, making no attempt to conceal his irritation and impatience. Minutes later, when they were in the car, a cream Range Rover, Scara observed drily 'Anyway, you should be happy about leaving that hole you call a room.'

'That's where I live, Scara,' Richard said, his face flaming. 'That's where I compose my music.'

'Ah, we've pricked the artist's sensitivity. Sorry.'

'Cut it out, Scara,' Keith said, 'the man is a comrade.'

Gaborone was still waking up. The streets were empty of traffic save for the occasional taxi ferrying a tourist to the Holiday Inn. The asphalt was wet, evidence of earlier rain, the early-morning sun cooking up steam. It was at this moment that Richard surrendered himself to the unknown, understanding that, as of then, his life didn't belong to him. He thought fleetingly of the women he was in the process of leaving, the few friends he had made among the Batswana. In his dealing with people, something had told him to discourage intimacy. He knew that he lived in a world where alliances were tenuous and friendships flickered on and off like a candle in a storm. The shebeen queens, though, would miss him, he had been a good if combustible customer.

Gama remembered his own journey from Lesotho to Angola, via Mozambique. How Mozambique was so different from anything in southern Africa: the loud *capulana* wraps women favoured over western-style dress, the ubiquitous soldier in fatigues cradling an AK-47, the billboards and posters sporting Samora Machel smiling benignly, the soft Portuguese syllables delivered in rapid staccato. The flight to Lusaka where the trainees were processed and then taken straight to TAAG airlines. The long haul to Luanda, a city which should always be seen from the air at night. The giant picture of Agostinho Neto at February the Fourth airport – and soldiers of Fapla, Fapla everywhere, a glimpse of the élite Red Berets, their boots treading on the soil for which so much blood had been spilt.

The camps themselves spoke of the battles that had been fought, the walls of barracks and the administration block pockmarked by bullets, much like walls of firing squads. The smell of cassava, the awesome sight of a baobab tree. Here men and women submitted to the authority of the administration and the instructors. Commands delivered in English, Spanish or Russian – and the singing that went on and on as people marched to their work detail. Gama pondered over today's preoccupation with the language question; how would the new South African National Defence Force deal with commands such as 'Attention!' or 'Fall in!' in eleven different languages? He laughed at himself, knowing that this was a preposterous idea. As he read on, he remembered a favourite song of the camp named after one of Angola's illustrious sons, Hoji ya Henda.

> *Tambo uyawabona lamabhun'esibulala*
> *singenacal'athumelen'uMkhonto*
> *Athumelen'uMkhonto*
> *uMkhonto we Sizwe*

the trainees would sing, an exhortation for Tambo first to look at the boers killing innocent people and then set uMkhonto we Sizwe loose upon them; singing, oblivious of the swarm of mosquitoes or bandit activity farther to the east of Malanje. Here, the children of South Africa enacted rituals which connected them to the heroes of the wars of resistance. Even if the training was hard and the instructors unyielding, something said to the trainees that, yes, they were part of a glorious legacy whose resolve would help liberate their bleeding land.

Richard took to training like a duck to water. Having finished the infantry course in Caculama, he was sent for further training to Moscow where he specialised in military combat work. Here, the instructors were hard, insisting on discipline. Even with all that, South Africans proved the truth of the maxim that you can take a *tsotsi* out of the township but you can't take the township out of a *tsotsi*. Some of the trainees managed to sneak out and carouse with buxom Russian women.

One trainee from Soweto railed against guard duty. *'Hoe kan die Russkies ons moet guard?'* he asked. *'Daar's baie Zulus hier, hulle moet guard. Hulle is a nation van mantshingelanas, mos.'* He maintained that the Zulus should be on guard duty since they were a nation of nightwatchmen.

Their training done, the South Africans graduated; some were sent straight to the GDR, Richard's group flew to Luanda via Lagos. He was amazed that, after all these intervening years, the airport was still named after Murtala Mohamed. The Nigerian leader had been assassinated in a go-slow.

Angola had also not changed much. Luanda showed that, even if the Portuguese had left in anger, the city was still stamped with their presence. Apart from Kimbundu and the *trocar*-friendly slang of the Zairos, Portuguese dominated in the tavernas, at the marketplace in Kinaxixi or during the celebration of May First, the *Dia do Trabalhador*. The colourful processions by OMA, the women's movement, and UNTA, the workers' organisation, constellated into a *festa* on the Primeiro de Maio plaza. Sometimes, Richard would come across Cuban troops in their aquamarine fatigues, their AKMs strapped across their backs. The Cubans never showed any strain of being far from home. It was in Luanda, at the ANC print-shop that was run by a Finn, Markku, that Richard came across Jonas Gwangwa again. Gwangwa was heavier and quieter – and walked with a limp. He had been injured in a car accident on the streets of Luanda after an Amandla performance. When the trombonist saw Richard, his face broke into this incandescent smile. After the two men had embraced, Gwangwa said, '*My laaitie, jy's so klein en jy's klaar 'n terroris* – you're so young and already you're a terrorist.'

Gama's remembrance of Angola and the role South Africans played was of a vast expanse of greenery, gigantic trees and untamed woods. The MK comrades were unlike any people he had ever come across; they were mostly uncomplaining about their lot. The long, long years in the camps. Malaria, which sometimes required that a camp functioned at half-strength. Then there were the rains that carried on interminably, making physical training a veritable torture. But in all this people maintained their humour. They sang their songs repeatedly, marching, laughing – sometimes crying – thinking of the day when they would finally lay down their heavy load. When Amandla visited some of the camps, it was carnival time. Gama remembered Richard when the group accompanied Tambo, who also acted as a conductor on special occasions. One such time was in October during the celebration of the Day of the Heroic Guerrilla. This was a ceremony of reaffirmation, a rallying of the troops. Richard looked gaunt, the saxophone seeming a heavy load in his hands. It was when he straddled the instrument and blew notes that had neither beginning nor end that it was clear that the man possessed and was possessed by his instrument. He blew with his head canted to the side as if waiting for a corroboration from the rhythm section. When it came, it was as if he had been pulled from a long and endless darkness onto steady ground.

Amandla toured several European capitals; they went to Brazil and returned with stories about women who were incredible.

In the ensemble, Richard had finally found a home. But this elation was short-lived. In 1984 a mutiny broke out and he was in the detachment assigned to defend Pango. It was the first time he had been involved in action; it dismayed him that this action was against his own people, no matter how misguided they might have been. For many nights, he thrashed and writhed under the assaults of nightmares, the images of bone shards, gristle and gore and brain tissue staying with him in all his waking hours. *Brother, brother,* he would sing in his head, *there's just too many of you dying …*

When the group went to Sweden, he had to remain because he was laid low with malaria. On recovering, he was told to pack his things. Then he was on a flight to Zambia, Lusaka. He worked with the Security Department, ensconced in Libala. It was in Lusaka that he met Nozi.

By Richard's own admission, Nozi was a woman brought by gods to save him from himself. Small and sinewy, Nozi challenged him when he was slack, encouraged him when he began to falter. She would laugh at him when he hummed for her snatches of tunes he had composed, her face transformed by her joy. Since she worked for the underground structures, they hardly had time together. The few moments they had, they enjoyed to the full. They decided to get married. The ceremony was at the Lusaka Civic Centre, where a slow-speaking Marriage Officer pronounced them man and wife. Nozi continued with her work, crossing the border from Botswana into South Africa. She set up dead-letterboxes for messages and arms caches. Then some of the comrades were captured, but Nozi managed to escape back to base.

It was in her eyes that he saw there was trouble. She remained in Lusaka for six months, and she was sure that she had been grounded. He was with her in 1989 when Walter Sisulu and seven other leaders were released from Robben Island. In January 1990, Nozi told him that she was again assigned to go inside. That night their lovemaking was full of sweetness tinged with unutterable pain. She held him as they rocked and rocked, both cursing the possibility of the hour of departure. As she cried out, Nozi gazed into his eyes as if engraving his face on the substrate of her memory.

A month passed without word from her. Then the ANC was unbanned and Nelson Mandela was released. Confusion reigned in Lusaka, where some of the comrades felt they had been left without direction. For those whose lives had depended on the continuation of the struggle, it was a moment of decision. Many applied to go to school, knowing that the future dispensation would have no role for them. Others girded their loins and readied for a long war of destabilisation which they knew the dying regime would wage. Richard was sent home in the same contingent with Oliver Tambo. He recalled the tumult at Jan Smuts Airport when the Old Man walked out of the Zambian craft, the women ululating, the workers pausing in the middle of serving, and running all the way to the tarmac. Then there was the Consultative Conference at Nasrec, the first sighting of Mandela. He could not express his joy.

He stayed in the country long after the conference, scouring township after township, knocking on doors, looking for Nozi. A year passed, then another. Even when the thought came that she might be dead, he banished it. For some reason, Richard was convinced that she would never die without giving him a sign.

By day he worked in the ANC Security Department at Shell House in Plein Street; by night he jammed with musicians in the city. This routine was interrupted by preparations for the elections. Day in and day out he worked with other cadres, visiting the flashpoints of violence, trying to bring sanity to communities that were certainly going off the rails. The elections came and went; at the victory celebrations at the Carlton Hotel, Richard, who wished Nozi were with him to share the moment of glory, got motherlessly drunk.

On the morning after election victory, Richard was still nursing an evil hangover when he heard a knock on the door. On opening, he saw two comrades; this filled him with a strange sense of *déjà vu*. 'Come in,' he said. His room was a mess.

One of the men, Steve, Richard knew, had worked in Ordnance. He was a tall Indian fellow with an infectious grin. Today he was quite grim. His partner, Tebogo, worked with the

Military Headquarters.

'Comrade Richard,' Steve said after sitting down, 'I guess we have some bad news for you.' He glanced at Tebogo, who was still standing, cradling a satchel. 'We've brought you some of Nozi's things.'

Richard experienced the kind of fear which left him numb. 'Where is she?'

'She's dead, Com,' Tebogo put in softly. 'We were with her in Special Ops. This was the time when we were in Natal. She was caught up in an ambush.'

'An ambush,' Richard echoed, failing to comprehend. 'Why wasn't I told?'

'It was difficult.' Steve's uneasiness increased. 'You see, at the time of her death she was under suspicion. One of the comrades had branded her, said she was working for the boers. I guess, her going out and trying to pull an operation single-handedly was her way of absolving herself.'

'But', Richard said, 'Nozi was a careful person. Surely, she couldn't just go out on a mission unprepared …?' He let the sentence trail off. When he next looked into their eyes, he saw a flicker, a subterranean message communicated by the two men. He was then hit by a realisation which left his mouth dry. 'Why don't you tell me the truth?' he asked. 'She was set up, wasn't she?'

'That's what we suspect,' Tebogo said. 'Comrades are still investigating. She must have been killed trying to find the real enemy agent in our unit. There are lots of people whose deaths still need checking. Unfortunately, at the moment people are still caught up in all these commissions.'

All these years. All these deaths. He thought of the sacrifices men and women had made; the betrayals which had led some of the best warriors in the land to a bloody end. Quite a few were interred in graves without headstones, unknown and unmourned in inaccessible sites.

'Sorry, Com,' Tebogo said with real tenderness. Then he handed a stunned Richard the satchel. 'This is where she kept her notes. I'm sorry that we had to read everything.'

'When did this happen?'

'In February 1990, just before they announced the unbanning of the Movement.' Steve seemed as if he were close to tears.

'Four years,' Richard said atonally. 'Four fucking years and you choose to tell me now ...' He couldn't remember when or how the two men left. He was in a daze for the whole day. In the afternoon, he ventured out of his Berea flat into scenes of jubilation. Thousands of people on the streets, even foreigners, all exulting in one of the greatest victories of the century. He went back inside, sat down and emptied the contents of the bag on the tangled sheets. Journals, notebooks. A letter in an envelope, dated simply 1990.

Dear Richard

I don't know where you are and in what frame of mind you might be when this letter reaches you, if it reaches you. I am all right in body and I guess that doesn't say much for my spirit. Certain things have happened here. I have been happy in my work and the comrades have been great. There is a small matter which all of us have to face as revolutionaries. It happens, now and then – and people sometimes pay a heavy price for this – that one falls under suspicion. In my case, I know that what is being whispered is not true. I love my country. I love the cause I have dedicated my life to serving.

There will possibly be a time when these nightmares will have become mere memory of a terrible chapter in the book of our life. Then I will tell you the whole story, or parts of the story because, who knows? No-one alive will ever know the whole truth. In the meantime, know that I love you and cherish you. I only wish that you will understand, sometimes, when things don't turn out the way we wanted them.

Love

N.

Richard flung the letter on the bed and howled and howled until his Mozambican neighbour broke down the door. They bundled him into a car and sped straight to Hillbrow Hospital. Since the doctors couldn't find anything physically wrong with him, they released him. By then he had lost the power of speech.

The phone rang. Gama heard the click as the machine answered. Then a voice: 'Hi, Leonard, it's Thembi. I hope you haven't forgotten –' Gama sprang to his feet and snatched the receiver from the cradle.

'Thembi, hi,' he said, speaking above Magriet's clipped syllables. 'Sorry about this. How are you?'

'I'm okay,' the disembodied voice said. 'What's with the answering machine? Skiving off today?'

'No such luck. No rest for the wicked.' He glanced at his wristwatch. 'Jesus. Is it four already? Tell you what. Why don't you wait for me at The Yard of Ale. Get a drink and I'll meet you there. Then we can see the exhibition.'

'Don't stand me up, Leonard Gama,' Thembi said, ' 'cause if you think you know wrath, you haven't experienced mine.'

'No, nothing like that. I need to talk to you.'

'Can't talk now, I suppose? Client confidentiality?'

'Something like that.'

'Okay. See you in a while.' The line went dead.

Gama pondered over the exchange, cursing himself for the arrangement with Thembi. He had told himself that it was nothing, a case of like-minded people coming together and enjoying each other's company. Women still made him uneasy, he could never be sure where he stood with them. There were many cases where he had thought that everything was on the level, and things had turned out otherwise. There were many women he had wounded. He certainly wanted to treat Thembi with respect, allow their friendship to bloom without complications. But then, he said to himself, Johannesburg had turned many a lonely person into a predator.

Stuffing Richard's papers into his attaché case, he switched off the lights and locked the office. On the way to the bank of lifts, he heard the booming of music from the adjoining studio. As he proceeded to the lift, he heard a sound not dissimilar to the whine of a distant mosquito; then four young men came out of the studio, singing in harmony. They were dressed in hip-hop gear and sported the high-top hair-do. These were to be the South African version of Boyz II Men. Gama admired their youthful enthusiasm. Nodding, he wished them luck. It was a tough world.

Richard temporarily forgotten, Gama concentrated on the road, giving the mini-bus taxis a wide berth. It was strange that these vehicles with bumper stickers proclaiming peace were driven by men not famous for peaceful activities. Just that afternoon, a mini taxi war had broken out in the city with a shoot-out in Bree Street, three dead. What amazed him was the resilience of the passengers who were squashed like sardines: what terrifying images went on in their minds? he wondered. But what really bothered him and raised his hackles was the lack of courtesy on the road, the big bozos in their German cars travelling at a hundred deaths an hour, cutting in front, only to be stopped by a red light. These should be exiled to Lagos, thought Gama, see how they deal with them go-slow apples. The idea of red-faced yuppies flailing their arms in the midst of an indifferent, treacle-slow traffic cheered him somewhat. That the traffic issue was a mess and public transport the pits could not be overstated. There was already a long queue on President Street, Friday people waiting patiently to get out of town. Poor Mac, Gama thought of what the Transport Minister had inherited. What does he make of all this?

As he pulled up into the parking area of the Market Theatre, he saw posters and banners announcing the opening of an art exhibition. Gama knew that art was supposed to play a part in therapy; how would he start introducing Richard to that regime? Immobilising the car before locking it, he scanned the late afternoon throng around the Market precinct. Wits-type men and women slumming it among the natives brushed shoulders with tourists who fought hard to disguise what they were. They were given away by their feet encased in grey socks under thong Jesus-style sandals, no different from cops in mufti being betrayed by their brown, size-eleven shoes. By their feet, Gama mused, ye shall know them.

The majority of the clientele patronising The Yard of Ale consisted of artists, playwrights, actors, singers and dancers. For members of the public, this was a favourite watering hole to visit while waiting for the shows to start. The atmosphere was usually pleasant, the drinks outdoors bringing to mind the pubs of London. Farther on along the paved area stood Kippies, which catered for the music lovers. It was closed today, for repairs. The gallery was next door to the pub; a knot of men and women in evening dress moved desultorily towards the entrance, invitation cards in hand. Gama espied Thembi at one of the tables near the door. She caught his eye and waved him over. She kept her eyes on him until he sat down across from her.

Although Thembi exhibited the confidence which came with her calm beauty, Gama knew that she could be very tentative in dealing with people. She was tall, angular – *My Masai princess*, Gama thought apropos of nothing – her height accentuated by her long neck. She wore her head in braids at whose ends was an assortment of coloured beads. Thembi was beautiful in that cold, distant manner discouraging to most men, with an ebony, chiselled face, large eyes and full lips which glistened with lip gloss. As she moved her hands, rows of gold bangles clattered; these set off her kaftan patterned in earth colours on a mother-of-pearl field. She regarded him with a mixture of kindness and humour.

'Hard day, huh?' she asked, taking a sip from a tall glass.

'You're telling me.' Gama looked round. At a table across, a lively discussion over the merits of a new lager was on. The occupants, in a slightly advanced state of inebriety, were united in their endorsement of the old lagers. This new stuff, someone put in, tasted like a horse's piss. A pregnant horse at that, another wit added. The hapless salesman, sobered by this harsh judgment, collected his cans to try his luck among drinkers some two tables away.

'Bet you're happy you're not that guy,' Thembi said. 'That's a *kak* way to earn a living, trying to introduce those jackasses to a new product ...'

'Maybe the guy's sales pitch stinks,' Gama said. 'South Africans might be creatures of habit, but they know a good thing when they see one.'

'Except in the Cape, of course,' Thembi said, trying to catch a waiter's attention. 'Those wouldn't know a good thing if it was served on a platter with their breakfast cereal. Shit, they made sure that Hernus Kriel became the only white *bwana* on the African continent.'

At first, Gama was puzzled by the bitterness in her tone until he remembered that Thembi was originally from Cape Town.

'Well,' Gama said, 'one day they'll remember District Six, and the vote that was taken away from them by the Nats. Maybe some will also remember with fondness all the callipers used to measure the breadth of the nose, and those pencils the boers shoved into their hair to determine whether or not they were white.'

'It's all that mountain air,' Thembi said, flicking her wrist dismissively. 'Maybe it's got chemicals which can turn activists into non-whites … ah, here comes the Messiah to deliver us from the drought.'

They placed their orders. While they waited for their whiskys, Thembi quizzed Gama on the progress of the divorce. It was a painful subject, one he would have preferred to avoid. But there was no side-stepping Thembi. She had a knack for extracting confessions that would have stood her in good stead with the Security Branch of yore. Briefly he told her that his wife was up in arms, wanting to take him to the cleaners, saying that he earned more than he had disclosed.

'Says I'm on the gravy train,' Gama said, shaking his head. 'If people really knew how much I get … it's sidewalk soup.'

'Thin sidewalk soup,' Thembi supplied, rearing her head and letting out a ripple of laughter.

'It's not funny.'

Their drinks came. Gama and Thembi toasted each other and listened to the silences inside themselves. The time came to go to the gallery. Inside, they found men and women resplendent in their finery, celebrating the undying tradition of art. The artist, a young man from Sebokeng, wore a white shirt under a blue blazer, a pair of grey slacks and a pair of trainers. He seemed ill at ease, not at all the flavour of the month. His paintings depicted scenes from everyday life in the troubled East Rand: barricades, the graffiti of hope and rage against a backdrop of burnt houses and blazing bodies. The critics and the art lovers were united in fulsome praise, all marvelling at the artist's un-erring eye for detail, strong lines and exquisite executions. The lights danced above the coiffured, moussed or permed heads of the gallery patrons, investing them with the fire which burnt in the young man's imagination. When Gama and Thembi came across him at the drinks table, he was tearing at chicken wings and washing them down with red wine. He confessed that he hadn't had a square meal in two days. He also had no transport. The two passed him a fifty-rand note. Thereafter, Thembi and Gama decided to tear themselves away from the appreciative crowd.

Later, they sat and ordered more drinks. The experience in the gallery had left them with a great disquietude. It was as if they had gazed upon a mirror which reflected all the unflattering aspects of their selves. Because, Gama asked himself, what have we done for the artists? For the Richards of the world who come and expose the more unpalatable features of our society and are then left alone to groan under the weight of discovery? We patronise them with exhibitions and gigs where they are paid paltry sums by a bloodless clientele which reaches an orgasm over a glimpse of how the other world lives. That other world does not live, it dies. It dies from the accumulated rage which renders it mute, where it sees the eyes of children without a future and women without hope begging on the streets, some with cardboard placards bearing the legend of the wretched. It lives in hospital wards where abused infants with broken limbs stare and stare in mute horror at the havoc adults are capable of wreaking.

'You're angry,' Thembi said. She covered his hand. 'Is it about the exhibition or is there something you wish to tell me?'

Gama felt on the verge of a breakdown. When he told her about Richard, he was actually telling her the story of his own life. He knew as he talked that he was also undergoing a therapy session that all South Africans, the guilty and the innocent, should undergo. Richard, he convinced himself, would be given the kind of occupational therapy befitting a musician. Gama saw the whole process unfolding before him, how music would be used to evoke memory and stimulate imagination. He would hold him, Richard, a brother, and tell him that there were people out there who loved him and who would make sure that, if he stumbled, they would hold him. Gama would remind Richard of his mother who had died while Richard was confronting himself in exile, and that, wherever she might be, she also loved him. There were many people, men and women, who would be there to walk the long road with him. The people would rejoice with him when a moment of joy presented itself, and they would weep with him, too, because Richard was of their flesh and their blood.

Some of the women, their walk and the way they carried themselves – the lilting laugh and the cadence of their speech – would remind him of Nozi. Gama would tell him that, yes, all the women involved in struggle are Nozi. They are there, these women, in the shacks of our country, trying to maintain their dignity in the face of abuses; they are there in hospitals, looking upon the eyes of men, women and children who have been ruined by disease and poverty. They are there, these women, singing their sad songs as they bury their loved ones cut down at a tender age by our collective cowardice. They will be there at the victory hour, when poverty and strife, pestilence and death are finally eradicated from our soil – and it is not a blasphemy to love them, but the highest tribute to Nozi's memory. Some of the sessions would be painful, as when he would let Richard re-experience the trauma, but he, Gama, would make him feel safe. We will play music together, he said to himself, and improvise. At the end, we'll let ourselves go.

Hot tears sprang into his eyes and streamed freely down his cheeks. Thembi leant forward and dabbed at his face with a tissue. 'Let's get to my place,' she murmured. Before he could respond, she shook her head. 'We don't have to do anything.'

The hubbub of drinkers and diners and the clink of glasses, the soft strains of piped music from somewhere inside the pub, the roar of traffic along Market Street punctuated by an angry blast of a hooter, the whispering wind which deepened the gathering of shadows and segued into the soft footfalls on the paved ground, the wail of a distant saxophone solo, the siren signalling the dawn of a new life or the dripping urgency of an expiring one, all cohered into a savage symphony of joy, a feature without which the Market region would die.

'Yes,' Gama said. 'Let's go.'

There Are Virgins
in the Township

Much like most human beings, it took me some time to settle comfortably in my trade. My reconciliation with my status as a journalist, that calling which, to many, does not require a lot of soul-searching nor lends itself to a lengthy contemplation of the moral navel, meant an acceptance on my part of a readiness to wound others.

Early in my career I recognised a flaw in my character, a ruthlessness born of my resolve to report and reflect and damn the consequences. In some quarters, this might charitably be interpreted as single-mindedness, a *sine qua non* for effective execution of tasks in hand, a necessary price to pay. In other circles, of course, where my words left a trail of squashed victims much like a snail's viscid emanation, my preoccupations defined themselves as nothing other than recklessness, a trespass against people's privacy and honour, or their notion of these virtues. Whichever way people interpreted my actions, my circle of friends was limited to the few members of the trade.

My elder brother Jonathan, on the few occasions he visited me in a succession of prison cells that were becoming my second home, would wax lyrical on the merits of friendship in our lives, something that all of us should nurture with every fibre in our bodies. He was fond of pointing out that there were many things happening in our country, with the new society striving to define its role. Many of those we regarded as friends tended to disappear, all using the excuse of being busy. For this reason, then, Jonathan would say, it would be foolish to alienate that small group who stuck by us and remembered us in their nightly prayers. I would listen to all this, my mind wandering, wishing for the appearance of a warder to terminate the harangue. Warders, like cops, are never there when you need one. On looking back, however, I see that he had a point. My discomfort with my brother, the fact that he was a Born Again Christian, did not diminish the gravity of his words. Now that he has disappeared, I miss him terribly. It is as simple as that.

Every person growing up in this country develops a sense of loyalty to friends and family. This is a primal instinct, as essential as breathing. In my case, however, friends and family were a crutch, a convenience which could be discarded at the onset of healing. I am certain that, given the opportunity, I would somehow have found a way of betraying them. In fact, I did betray my parents. They had high hopes for me, seeing me through school and encouraging me to become a lawyer or a doctor, that is, respectable, a credit to the race. I was loth to study, preferring to immerse myself in the picaresque adventures of characters peopling novels by Peter Cheyney or James Hadley Chase, the racy contraband nestling safely behind an exercise book.

My best friend, Arthur Sikhosana, marvelled that I managed to pass at all. It is worth mentioning here that, even with this cavalier attitude to education, I was always at the top of the class. In retrospect, it must be said that it was exactly this disposition which made my education possible. Had I conscientiously swallowed all that Bantu Education bilge which was our daily fare, I would have ended up in a madhouse.

During Standard Four, my English compositions were routinely read to the Standard Six classes, as examples of fine writing, the teachers were wont to say. Even then, I knew – I could sense – that the teachers were somewhat disappointed with my academic performance. They could divine that I had it in me to do better, be a credit to our beleaguered race, and scale loftier heights. I had no intention of being a credit to anybody. As for scaling loftier heights, climbing up a telephone pole and daring others to follow me was enough, thank you. Being good was bad. School was a vehicle for greatness, sure, for success – whatever these meant to an adolescent – but I wasn't going to kill myself or turn myself into a freak in pursuit of excellence.

It is possible that my sense of unease with greatness and a mistrust of success charted the path I would follow later in life. I had seen many a great man falter and fall from dizzy heights – and how the people who had thrust them to greatness rejoiced at the inelegance of their collapse.

A case in point was our Principal. Mr Sithole, a strict disciplinarian and lay preacher, was also a closet alcoholic. We knew his secret, having heard him being roasted by a shebeen queen one month-end. His final fall from grace, however, came when one evening he drank himself into such a state that he couldn't tell the toilet from his seventy-year-old father's bedroom, where the hapless old man woke up to a shower of urine. From that day on, Mr Sithole Senior slept swathed in an outsize anorak. 'What do you do', he asked philosophically, 'when your son gets so pissed he doesn't know where to direct his pippie?'

At thirteen, my own pippie was stirred by the sight of girls in our school. I was also popular with them, this strange breed being eternally attracted to young men of my ilk who revel in teetering at the edges of precipices. I feared girls and was envious of the freedom in their femininity. The best camouflage, a carapace I wrapped around me, was to make myself as unappealing as possible. Where the other boys vied for Florsheim shoes, grey Barathea slacks and button-down Viyella shirts, I adopted the fashion of slobs: scuffed and loose-laced Bata shoes, baggy trousers and creased shirts. I popped gum loudly, hawked and spat insolently and never hid the fact that I was a smoker. The more I treated the girls with scorn, the more they sought out my company. This perceived ease with which I operated in the world did not endear me to quite a few of my schoolmates; they felt it unfair that this delinquent bested them without seeming to raise a sweat.

Only Arthur Sikhosana, my childhood friend and neighbour, stood by me through these moments of adolescent madness, sometimes earning the wrath of his father in the process. When I was detained in 1976, it was he who campaigned relentlessly for my release; our friendship spans more than two decades, from the heyday of repression when there was an open season on black people, and black flesh was sweet to the palates of police dogs, through the halcyon days of transition where death was as commonplace as mushrooms after a thunderstorm, to this heady new dispensation. It is with this background, then, that what happened between Arthur and me deserves more than a passing comment.

Arthur and I – or, rather, our families – came to KwaMashu around the same time. His mother and father and two elder sisters moved from Mkhumbane, a shantytown which was a precursor of today's squatter camps. His father drove a Durban Corporation truck; his mother worked for some white people in Ridge Road. We had become victims of the Group Areas Act in Mayville. This meant that we had to make way for white people; KwaMashu was the Promised Land. I still remember Jonathan's grim face when we unloaded our belongings from the lorry which had bumped and groaned under the heavy weight. It was when I looked at the clutter of household goods strewn on the ground, within a perimeter that was demarcated by wooden pegs, that I realised that families could certainly accumulate a lot of garbage. While my father was being helped by neighbours to move the furniture into the box-like four-roomed house, my mother sat on a grass mat, looking at the dust swirling behind the disappearing lorry, her face as eloquent as the ages.

It was perhaps in her eyes that I read a message regarding our lives. She tried to make Jonathan and me forget our previous life in Mayville, the rambling house which adjoined our father's church, and our Indian friends, Manilal and Premlal Parboo, with whom we wrestled near the dam, where we played childhood games, all oblivious of what the State had in store for us.

Jonathan was a quiet boy; this caused my parents a lot of anxiety. His dreamy expression meant, for them, that he would become a visionary or a criminal. I was not a problem. As soon as I got to KwaMashu, I reconnoitred the streets, made friends easily and got up to the usual mischief. Arthur was always there, deferring to me in most cases, fighting my battles if the need arose. He was the first boy of eight I knew who owned dogs. He really loved the animals, sometimes purring and addressing them in soft tones as if they were human, threatening us with mayhem if we kicked them. For my part, I didn't see their use. These were just mangy mongrels which made a nuisance of themselves by upsetting dustbins.

Arthur and I ran each weekday to school, the ink bottle and a leather-bound Bible knocking about in each of our suitcases. Although we didn't share a desk, it was known that he was my best friend. He was bigger than I, so I could needle the other boys, comfortable in the knowledge that, if trouble came, he would be there to sort them out.

He was, however, not just a gentle, overgrown kid. Arthur would participate in youthful shenanigans with glee. But he seemed to maintain a certain distance from any messy development. I suspect, now, that he actually initiated some of the capers. During holidays we stole into the churchyard and picked mangoes and guavas, all the time watching for the priest's dogs. If they came upon us, Arthur had a way of pacifying them. I reasoned then that dogs probably took to fat kids. Since I was skinny, I imagined that the dogs were attracted to my barely hidden bones.

Part of growing up included working during school holidays. We were not poor, and my mother worried that I would get into more trouble in 'town', as the downtown area of Durban was known. She didn't trust me alone, or with a group of like-minded boys in the concrete and asphalt jungle which had claimed so many. But, working while a student meant that one got some experience of the real world. It was Arthur's intervention which saved the day. He convinced my mother, I later learnt, that dirtying my hands would make me a more wholesome human being. It was Arthur, also, who benefited more than all of us put together.

We worked in the scullery of a large departmental store. When not wrestling with grime, we were required to serve in the kitchen, spreading a mix of vanilla essence with white Stork margarine on slices of bread. This fare was for the African canteen. In the Indian, White and Coloured canteen, people had their tea or coffee with genuine buttered toast. Young as I was, the country's preoccupation with colour, with putting each na-

tional group in a specific pigeon hole, did not escape me. Arthur
negotiated for me to be put in his detail, which loaded tripe,
pieces of fish, sandwiches and Russian sausages onto aluminium
trays. The trays were then installed on a trolley which we
wheeled downstairs to the general factory area. Workers came
and bought. Since all the food items were entered into a note-
book by an Indian chef, Reddy, I took it for granted that there
was nothing illegal about the operation. Much later I realised
that the figures that Reddy entered didn't tally with the number
of items in the trays. What Arthur was doing was to double or
treble the amount of goods and then give Reddy a false count.
Reddy didn't check, such activity was beneath him. When I
caught Arthur out, he agreed to share the spoils. In fact, he organised another trolley. 'These people', he said – meaning Reddy,
the white administration, representatives of the whole unjust
world – 'are robbing us blind. Just look at the prices on these
things, it's daylight robbery.' I couldn't argue with that logic. It
vindicated the little robbery of our own. Arthur also rose in my
estimation.

After these adventures, we returned to school cockier, more
knowledgeable about the ways of the world. We drifted further
and further from our parents, or from the methods they used to
combat the hostile white world.

The first time Arthur and I started having differences – a time
which I should have considered with great care – was over
Zodwa, who was without doubt the most beautiful sixteen-year-
old at Isibonelo High School.

I was sixteen then, going on seventeen. I had fooled around
with members of the opposite sex but, as I have said before, my
relationship with girls, dubious and troubled as it was, was
strictly on my own terms. Zodwa, however, seemed totally oblivious of my antics; perhaps – and this is twenty-twenty hind-
sight – they amused her, but she was certainly not fooled. To
add to my worries, Arthur began to stay back after school and
it was clear that he had designs on her. I then hit on a plan.

'Arthur,' I said one afternoon, 'I think Zodwa is in love with
you.'

'What?' he asked. 'G'wan, you. I've seen the way you've been ogling her.'

'No, Arthur. Seriously. I heard her talking to Maisie. She really thinks you're a dish.' This was all bullshit, of course. Zodwa never said anything of the sort. In fact, Maisie had confided in my current girl-friend that *she* rather fancied Arthur. A bit of a laugh, really, since Maisie had a tendency to balloon out as if at will. That she carried a torch for Arthur was a subject that drove some of the more unsympathetic students to hysterics; it was tantamount to being fancied by a Goodyear blimp.

I advised Arthur to pursue Zodwa. She was not a common township girl who was mesmerised by flashy cars and meretricious goods. The best route to her heart was via an understanding of her interests. Later, as we hung out on the verandah of Mashiphela's store or under the shade of an umdoni tree, Arthur would tell me about Zodwa. She loved a simple life, going to church, listening to music and reading. While this research was going on, I conducted my own probe. I attached myself to the shift which cleaned the Staff Room, ensuring my access to the cabinets storing student files. I was thrilled at the discovery that her birthday was on 29 May; since it was then the beginning of April, I had about three weeks to perfect my plan.

A certain fever grips Durban during the Easter period. Even though our parents were strong believers – my mother going to church every Sunday in her blue two-piece tunic, the jacket adorned by a white crocheted scarf, and my father looking as grim as an undertaker in his black suit and dog collar – I still couldn't quite grasp the reason for the big to-do over the death of Christ. One of the highlights of the Easter celebrations was the Passion Play. The tickets, as they say here, were as scarce as an Indian policeman in Bloemfontein. For quite a vast section of the black population, attending this performance was out of the question. It was not a racial thing; even the most rabid segregationists could not afford the stigma that would attach to them if they barred black people from the City Hall. Moreover, the company this year had threatened to suspend the one and only appearance in the city if black audiences were prohibited. The show was usually booked out months in advance.

My anxiety about how to get the tickets was solved by the

timely intervention of James Firth, a clergyman who was my father's superior. When he visited, I offered to wash his car which was parked in the street. Firth gazed at me from the depths of his blue eyes, possibly thinking that I wanted to hit him for a church bursary. After the obligatory prayers followed by gallons of tea, he made to bid us goodbye. As he moved up the steps to the street, I told him that, as part of an assignment, I was supposed to write about Easter celebrations, and how I had tried to get tickets to the Passion Play but to no avail. Whether he believed this cockamamie story or not I can't tell. But he arranged for me to pick up the tickets from his secretary at the Christian Assemblies Church headquarters on Smith Street.

I remember very little of the play except that it terrified me. This is where I saw the difference between theatre and cinema; here were real people made of flesh and blood, their presence as palpable as Zodwa's clammy palm in my hand. It was easy, then, to understand why some people were weeping in the audience. The journey to Golgotha, for me, anyway, started looking quite real. It represented the hardships, the pain, which people endured every day. Zodwa tightened her grip when they laid down David Horner, the crowned actor who played Christ. She winced at each hammer blow as the nails were driven into Horner–Christ's hands and feet. When I looked at her, she was crying, tears rolling down her face. When the play ended to a rousing chorus, I was myself on the verge of weeping.

The night outside was balmy, rain waiting in the clouds for the famous Durban downpour. The people came out and rushed to their cars. Couples walked, hand in hand, as if the experience inside the theatre had strengthened their commitment to each other. As we walked down the wide street which was being constructed into a one-way, amber lamps shone upon us, on the people, removing whiteness from white faces and investing black people with a regal hue. Here and there policemen stood in twos or threes as if watching out for the beginning of a riot, their eyes shadowed by visored caps. We passed one minion of the law holding an Alsatian that strained against its leash. I looked up at the policeman's eyes. Under the light they were the loneliest, bleakest eyes I had ever seen, cold and grey as cut glass.

As we sat in the Putco bus that was bound for KwaMashu, Zodwa, having composed herself, looked me straight in the eye. 'Do we tell Arthur about this?'

'Why do you ask?'

'Because you know he wants me to be his girl.' She was quiet for a while, looking at the play of light and shadow on the shrubbery outside. She turned her eyes to the scattering of late-night passengers in the bus. 'Isn't that what it is? You're his friend, aren't you, Bobo?'

Instead of answering, I asked her, 'Do you want to be his girl?'

'I don't know.' She swallowed. My princess swallowed. I couldn't take my eyes off her, she was a dream, soft skin the colour of good coffee, eyes as black as night, and lips that seemed to retain their softness even as she nibbled at them with her lower teeth. 'Arthur is . . . so proper. The kind of guy a woman would like to get married to one day.'

I felt an unreasoning flash of anger against Arthur. He had no right to intrude, not now.

The bus rolled on. Somewhere up front a radio was playing *mbaqanga*, Mahlathini singing, '*Sengikhala ngiyabaleka*', a group of boys in Wanderers Football Club strip singing along. An old, grey-bearded man in white Zion Christian Church robes got on, followed by a group of women in blue. They sat three or four rows in front. The man stood up and started preaching, railing against the sins of the flesh. I thought of telling Zodwa that some of these men were really fast with women, but thought that would offend her. Zodwa sighed. 'My stop is coming now,' she said. Before I could say anything, she leant forward and gave me a fleeting kiss on the lips. 'Thank you for taking me out. I enjoyed the play.' She stood up. 'I'm not used to scheming, Bobo. But if you don't say anything to Arthur, neither will I.'

I made to stand up to walk her home. She placed a hand on my shoulder. 'Don't worry. I'll be okay. I don't want my folks to see you – not yet.' Then she walked unsteadily down the aisle.

The bus pulled to a stop. I saw her walking towards the path leading to her house in E section. I thought she would turn and wave, but she walked on until she disappeared around a corner. That night, I went to sleep with the memory of Zodwa's kiss on my lips.

My brother Jonathan was concerned. 'You must be careful, Bobo. You've learnt to play this game where you set the rules. But comes a time when you have no power and people come and play your game and you lose. You must never take people for granted. Never underestimate their thirst for revenge.'

'But Arthur is a friend, Jonathan.'

'That's even worse.'

If Arthur knew that I was seeing Zodwa, he never let on. We were still friends, although he was now given to long moments of silence. Schools closed for the winter holidays. Arthur went to his relatives in Mkhuze; I continued seeing Zodwa in what was now a full-blown affair. She took me to meet her father, who hated me on sight. That wasn't surprising. Then she changed schools and was sucked up in the maw of a girls' college in Pietermaritzburg.I wrote her several letters which came back unopened with a RETURN TO SENDER stamp across the envelope. I was wounded by this, I who had never tasted rejection. What was even more hurtful was that I couldn't share my predicament with Arthur. Eighteen months later I was kicked out of the University of Fort Hare after a sit-in. Arthur persevered at the University of Zululand, where he completed his B.Sc.

When I came across him at the Indian Market on Victoria Street, he had changed. I was kicking around at the Banner News Agency, stringing for an assortment of Durban newspapers. The hours were long and the pay scandalous. Arthur was now a serious person, aiming at becoming a geology lecturer. I knew that, even if he showed happiness at meeting with me again, something about my condition must have embarrassed him. Seeing him compounded my sense of failure. I knew then that if I was not going to spend the rest of my life wallowing in self-pity, I needed to excel in something. And since journalism was beckoning, I had to make my mark there.

Two months later, Arthur came to my parents' funeral; mother and father had been killed in a car crash in Pinetown. Our heads were shorn of hair, as was the custom, so that death and shaving have become closely associated in my mind. The few uncles and aunts – and a whole battery of cousins – did their best to comfort us. But the pain, the loss, were there, and it was only with their death that I realised how little I knew of my mother and father. What had been their dreams? What had occupied their thoughts, nightly, as they replayed in their minds the events of the day? Because, in those days, every opportunity to go to sleep was an act of defiance, of resistance. I knew that they had loved each other, sometimes to the point where each was interchangeable with the other, my father usually misplacing his spectacles and wearing mother's to read the paper or his Bible, my mother padding into the kitchen, looking smaller in father's terry-cloth bathrobe.

While Jonathan slumped deeper and deeper into depression, Arthur and I were inside the tent, finishing off a bottle of whisky. In a drunken daze I remembered him saying something about Zodwa, and that he was now married and his wife was expecting. I promised to call on him and see his family.

But by that time I was following a lead on corruption in the South African Broadcasting Corporation. In its propaganda against the African National Congress, white radio writers created virulently anti-communist serials which were translated by blacks into African languages. One translator, Themba Nguni, evidently sick and tired of this charade, slipped some liberation movement comment into one play. Knowing that the Special Branch would be knocking at dawn, Nguni went straight to our newspaper and sought me out.

They detained him under Section 6 of the Suppression of Communism Act. But I had a story under my belt. All that was needed was corroboration from other translators. The SABC building was guarded and entry was difficult. I posed as a successful job applicant called in for an interview. I managed to collect a lot of dirt on what some of the Calvinist, churchgoing copy-tasters deemed morally acceptable for black people. In some offices, too, men read pornographic magazines and indulged in bacchanalian raillery. All this was kept under a tight lid. I filed my story and waited for the storm.

It came at 4 a.m. in the form of one Warrant Officer Pelser, who, accompanied by two African Security Branch officers as eager as retrievers, took me to the Fisher Street Security Police headquarters. After the obligatory physical and verbal abuse, I was transported to a number of police stations. Jonathan, who was now a minister of religion, gained entry. It was here that he preached to me. Arthur came too. This was strange because a detainee was not supposed to have visitors. I suppose the police thought that my brother or my friend would talk me out of what was called communist nonsense.

But by then I was no mere newsman; I had become news. My colleagues joined in the campaign for the release of detainees. My name made the headlines. I was released nine months later, without being charged.

I was offered a senior editorship, but by then I was being wooed by the *Rand Daily Mail* in Johannesburg. I worked for them until the paper folded under the pressure of greater market imperatives. It was then that Mark Kastner offered me a job with *The Herald*. I couldn't resist the call.

Five years after Mandela's release, I found myself back in Durban. My city of birth also became the arena of my undoing. It is strange how a mundane thing such as the death of someone you might have known as a kid – and possibly not liked – can impact on your life. And how, if you had not gone to a particular event you might not have met someone who contributed to changing the course of your life. Thomas Manzi's death had this influence on me.

I remember Thomas Manzi as a fierce roughhouse type of schoolboy who talked back to the teachers and harassed us for the few cents of pocket money our parents had given us. I would hear much later that after the June 1976 Soweto Uprising, when young people skipped – the parlance of that dreadful hour for exile – Manzi's parents were so fed up with him that they asked him if he hadn't seriously considered skipping the country. If school was tough, Thomas made it unbearable. If he sat next to you in class, for instance, your fate was sealed. The teachers, especially Mr Zondi who taught us Geography, had this terrible habit of posing difficult questions. If no hand shot up, he would thrash the whole class with a cane. Thomas believed in someone sacrificing for the collective; when Zondi asked a question, Thomas would stick the sharp point of his Three Star blade into your elbow, causing the hand to jerk up involuntarily, resulting in the teacher pointing at you, the brilliant solver of mysteries, saying, 'Yes, Bobo? What is an isthmus?', Isthmus? Isn't that what your toothless grandmammy lisps when she wants to say "Christmas"?' You would babble some nonsense and of course get caned. It was unfair. Who, doing Standard Five, under Bantu Education, besides, knew what an isthmus was?

So here I was entering the church at Thomas's funeral. I was still mulling over his death, looking for a place to sit, when a voice said: 'Well, well. If it isn't old Bhongoza himself . . .'

Now, I really hate it when someone calls me 'Bhongoza'. My name is Bobo, no more, no less. However, I controlled myself, ignored the greeter and concentrated on the throng in the church. It was a motley crowd, taxi drivers taking a breather in between taxi-wars, church women in the red and white strip of the Methodist Church, this holy side for God, some musicians who lugged their instruments waiting for the moment when they would be required to play, and general hangers-on. Honoured guests moved silently to the platform, led by a priest. Family members sat in the front pews. The casket stood on a bier, wreaths and fresh flowers covering the top, a section of flowers arranged into a message, WE LOVE YOU DAD.

'Hey, Bobo, my bro,' the man behind me persisted, 'how are you?'

This time I turned slowly, composing my face into a smile of feigned surprise. It was Arthur Sikhosana. Balding profusely and almost visibly growing fatter, Arthur was still the same boy whose girl I had stolen some twenty years ago. He wore an expensive-looking dark suit, a white shirt clasped at the collar by a black bowtie and black patent leather shoes. The bowtie had an effect of separating his bullet-head from the rest of the body. It took me a while to realise that Arthur's companion, a plump, handsome woman who hovered restlessly around him while clutching a handbag close to her body, was actually Zodwa. She knew that pickpockets were not loth to ply their trade among mourners. Just recently, there had ensued a hue and cry in Munsieville, Klerksdorp, when one of the more nimble-fingered tsotsis made off with a gold wedding ring which some lax mortician had left on the finger of the deceased.

When I saw Zodwa, I felt a pang of guilt, but it was guilt mixed with great relief. Something had changed her from a sharp, self-possessed young woman into a matron of shabby respectability. I knew that what I had done to them was the bottom of the moral totem pole. Both had trusted me at one stage of our lives and I had let them down. Their faces, however, expressed nothing which could have been interpreted as antipathy. Arthur still looked as if he wanted to continue where we had left off, wherever that was, and Zodwa's face was composed, as unreadable as a blank page.

'Arthur,' I cried, spreading my arms wide but still hoping that he wouldn't embrace me, 'what a surprise!'

'Meet my wife, Zodwa.' Arthur shrugged as if introducing his wife was an unpleasant but necessary task. 'This is my old buddy, Bobo. You must remember Bobo?' His smile broadened; Zodwa looked bewildered. From that introduction, I knew that Arthur had known of our little liaison, and that it had hurt him. I wondered whether he would ever forgive me.

I grinned and mumbled a greeting. Arthur steered us to a pew with a sprinkling of mourners. However hard I tried to manoeuvre myself away from the couple, Arthur skirted around and insinuated his bulk beyond the seated people so that I found myself wedged in between the Sikhosanas. I hate funerals as a rule; this one was definitely not going to be a bundle of giggles either. Feeling the warmth of Zodwa's thigh pressing against the fabric of her skirt, I wondered what she was thinking. I remembered those thighs when they were still supple, wrapped around my waist, shit, this was neither the time nor the place to have these thoughts. I had to concentrate on why I was here, my mission.

The service mercifully over, I followed Arthur as we filed out of the church. When we got outside, an easterly wind was rising, ruffling the leaves on treetops, carrying in it a promise of rain. Cushiony clouds scudded across a sky against which swallows flying in formation were framed. Somewhere far, in one of the township houses a dog barked, to be followed by the plaintive wailing of a child.

Spectators drawn to the hearse stood in ragged groups, some leaning against parked cars. Men took off their hats as eight pallbearers emerged out of the gloom of the church and installed the casket in the hearse. Thomas's girlfriend, Tozi, looking crushed and desirable and infinitely alone, nodded at the attendant who held the limousine door open for her. She entered and sat down. The door clicked shut, a mere whisper of steel against chrome. Then the cortège began its slow movement to the cemetery, the young choristers in black and blue gowns following the procession, stepping in time to the measured tread of the attendant, who wore striped trousers, a swallowtail coat, an Ascot tie and a top hat. The number of German cars confirmed the late Manzi's popularity among the more affluent of the land. Indeed, I couldn't help overhear two urchins standing and gawping with admiration. 'Check that Dolphin,' one said, pointing at a burgundy BMW, 'a gravymobile for amaGents!'

'So how is Jo'burg treating you?' Arthur asked, not really expecting a reply, pouring me a shot of scotch. We were in his house at D Section. As I tasted the amber liquid, feeling it course down my stomach, I pondered over the day's events. They were fraught with subterranean meanings which portended a darkness that I would have a hard time conquering. It could have been pure exhaustion, or the effect of alcohol, but I experienced a momentary flash, a vision, where I saw a great boulder rolling towards me, my mind screaming, *Move, you fool!* while my limbs defied the command. I fought off an urge to scream, knowing that this was not actually happening. On opening my eyes, I found Zodwa staring at me with a fierce intentness. Shaking myself out of this seizure, I excused myself and went out of the lounge.

'You okay, bro?' Arthur asked, soon standing behind me as I looked at the rain falling on his flower garden. Behind us the small, dark speakers of his expensive CD player issued sweet soul music. When I turned to look at him he was walking back to the kitchen. Zodwa sat paging through a magazine, her legs folded under her body, her shoes on the carpet. Since the door separating the lounge from the kitchen was open, my eyes were drawn to the wood panelling, the pine units and the gleaming aluminium sink. Arthur, having discarded his sombre suit for a loose cardigan, jeans and slippers, was bent in half, his arms working.

I walked back to the sofa and prepared to engage Zodwa in conversation, dreading the prospect, for, really, what was there to talk about? There was just too much to talk about. The music played on, amid this profound silence, bringing into the room an ethereal, sorrowful mood; this was deepened by the singing of many voices that were laden with nostalgia and sadness and regret for countless transgressions. These anonymous young singers who raised their voices in praise of an unknown god and who evoked an unseen power, pushed me deeper into the softness of the sofa, a lump in my throat.

A soft, satisfied growl from the kitchen heralded the appearance of a large labrador. It was the dog Arthur must have been stroking when he was bent like that in the kitchen. He continued to caress the animal, his own tone low and soft as he murmured words of endearment. I looked up from the dog and saw Zodwa gazing at the pet with a look of such malevolence it could only have sprung from long pent-up feelings. I understood, as if in a moment of religious revelation, that it was on the dog that Arthur lavished his affection. Zodwa was part of the furniture, an untouched bauble that would be summoned to grace occasions which called for such appearances of respectability. All this communicated to me that she must be an extremely lonely woman indeed. An earlier guilt returned; in not acknowledging what had happened between us, I had effectively put Zodwa at Arthur's mercy, where she was treated like a shopsoiled article, of no account. I felt the weight of what we men do to put women at a disadvantage, where we blaspheme those intimate moments of love and codify them as conquests – we, the eternal swordsmen – while they retreat, maimed, to lick their wounds in that most private, unreachable corner of their hearts.

As Zodwa's eyes softened and misted, Arthur raked us with his own, triumphant that he had finally reached his destination in life: a car, a house, a wife, a dog and freedom. The dog, possibly sensing the tension in the room, gave a cough, then padded to the rug spread near the drinks cabinet. Arthur's movements were now slower and more deliberate, much like a drinker wishing to dispel the impression that he or she is getting sozzled. I have had many experiences with drinking people and I know that when the intake reaches a certain level – especially if there is a little unpleasant issue to be resolved – people can be unpredictable. I knew that it was time to leave. As if seeking to thwart my intention, Arthur picked up the bottle and poured out two measures of whisky into the glasses. 'Top up, bro?'

'Do you see much of Jonathan?' I asked, suddenly feeling a great urge to see my brother.

'Ja, a while back,' Arthur said, 'we collided at one of these Movement do's. He was in the organising committee for Tambo's visit to King's Park.'

'I thought he wanted nothing to do with politics?'

'You'll be surprised how many people have changed.' Arthur regarded his glass, swirling the liquid within. 'There are those we call the six-month wonders, who joined the ANC six months before elections, when it was quite clear which way the cat would jump.' He sipped his drink and twisted his lips. 'It's funny. It's exactly those people who landed cushy government jobs. But Jonathan was in it from the very beginning.'

'Jonathan?' I couldn't visualise my staid, religious brother running errands in the execution of the liberation struggle.

'It's true.' Arthur sounded distracted as if this conversation conflicted with some voice which spoke from inside himself. Then he smiled, urbane and controlled. 'What say we take a drive. Get some air?'

'Have you visited your parents' graves, Bobo?' Zodwa asked. It appeared to me that this was the question she had been waiting to ask the whole afternoon. Arthur turned his eyes to her, favouring his wife with a look which must have been on Balaam's face when the ass challenged him.

I shook my head. The prospect certainly didn't appeal to me.

I feared the things such a visit would evoke in me. When Arthur nodded and said that this was a good idea, I felt like someone participating in a game with arbitrary laws, where winning was losing and vice versa. I sat thinking of the dread possibility of being rebuked for neglecting a son's duty. At the same time, I had a feeling of being swept along with schemes which had been hatched long before my arrival in this house. I thought of Jonathan and, without being told, I knew that this couple had actually been supporting him financially, if not spiritually. Which meant that they were paying rent for the house I had left, my father's house. With this sense of shame then, I gathered my briefcase and left the comfort of my seat. While Arthur went to get his car keys, I approached Zodwa and hugged her, taking in the faint whisper of her perfume and hair lotion. She held me tight and I remembered the strength of her clasp, then pushed me away. I had a feeling that she would later go into the bathroom and wash away the memory of our contact. '*Hamba kahle*, Bobo,' she said, 'and may your gods be with you.' The dog watched us with brown, baleful eyes.

I hesitated at the door. 'Maybe we can talk some time?'

'We'll never talk again, Bobo,' Zodwa said in a fierce whisper. 'Not now, not ever!' In a gesture of dismissal, she bent over the machine. There was a soft hiss as the disk tray slid forward. Zodwa replaced the disk with something upbeat, a tune which both summoned our past and said farewell to whatever had taken place between us. It was a disavowal of any part she had played before, an embrace of whatever the future would offer.

Sunday people, the drunks and the holy believers, brought back the ghosts from the past. We passed them on the streets, my people, moving in a narcotised stupor, their form of dress signifying the crutch of their choice. Women in yesterday's party clothes speaking in harsh, whisky-scarred tones, their partners accompanying them in sullen silence. The men looked dangerous in their suits and hats and shoes that still gleamed in the gathering dusk. Somewhere from inside a house, a snatch of loud music and revellers' voices. Some men, women and children under a bus shelter, the young men's eyes defiant, disconsolate and full of longing.

We hit F Section where blackened ruins had replaced a shopping centre, speaking of battles that had raged in pre-election days. This was where we danced the latest township jive, smoked the first joint and harassed our first girl. Scrub now abounded in a space formerly occupied by a community centre.

The smell wafting into the car from the street was a smell I remembered from my own youth. Flowers fought exhaust fumes, the eternal struggle of life against death. Although many houses were now electrified, you still came across smoke from wood- or coal-burning stoves billowing out of asbestos chimneys. Hibiscus hedges and bougainvillaea-fronted houses, while giant rubber trees kept a silent watch over the street.

On Zulu Road, an impi of about forty men dressed in traditional attire danced and beat their shields with knobkerries. This was an exuberant crowd, perhaps from an *imbizo*, a convocation of subjects in a chief's kraal. Instead of people scattering – the healthiest response to armed men – they stood watching, little children pointing at pot-bellied men whose fleshy folds flowed over loin-skins. Some women ululated, urging the prancing warriors on, reliving in their minds the glories of past kingdoms. Since I had covered countless violent incidents involving these warriors' kinsmen, I was surprised at feeling unthreatened as we negotiated our way through this vibrant throng. Looking at the rippling muscles on the bare torsos of some of the younger men, I felt over-dressed and stupid, alien in my Western clothes. I also knew that, second to people involved in struggle, there is nothing more beautiful than people engaged in the celebration of their culture.

We passed my old high school, now bordered by a high barbed-wire fence, the windows burglar-proofed and covered with wire mesh. Weeds and green saplings grew in stubborn abundance around the building, this neglect speaking of a greater inclination on the part of the community to let things go. It was with a mixture of sadness and rage – an emotion which grips one on leaving a hospital after a necessary amputation – that I turned my eyes away from the school which had shaped us and maimed us in equal measure. So many of my classmates were gone, claimed by the streets to become pale imitations of their former selves. Some had found meaning in the struggle, and many more had entered the never-never-land where they nightly pursued the dream of the everlasting rand note.

In the approaching dark, we took the narrow, untarred road to the cemetery. The air smelled of growth, wood-smoke and lumber. Even as we alighted from the car, hearing the call of night birds and frogs croaking in hidden wetlands, I knew that I had been summoned to this terrain by something much bigger than ourselves. Arthur walked beside me in silence. His breath came out in short pants, providing a counterpoint to the raw-edged rising wind. Shadows in the twilight invested the area with strange shapes where the sighing wind carried within itself the unwhispered secrets of the dead.

I followed Arthur to a canopy of wattle where the darkness deepened. It felt as if we had been walking for miles. My skin prickled as I stepped on something soft and squelchy, perhaps a dead rodent, before a feral smell rose and assailed my nostrils. In this dark, which was the most absolute of nights, I was revisited by that epiphanic moment of earlier in the day. What had been straining for expression, something that had been hidden so deeply within the folds of my consciousness, burst forth, unsummoned. I knew, then. Before I could speak, there was a soft snick! of a pistol being cocked. Just then, the clouds above parted and a pale moon gleamed like a polished silver coin. Arthur, his eyes shadowed, stood in the light with the gun hand hanging parallel to his legs.

You must never take people for granted. Jonathan's words echoed from the dead and unburied past. I took a step forward. Arthur lifted the pistol and pointed it at the region of my chest. He was wheezing like an old man. Strange as this may sound, I was not afraid.

'He's dead, isn't he, Arthur?' I asked the question, not really expecting an answer. 'You killed him. Jonathan. Didn't you?'

'Your brother seduced my wife, Bobo,' Arthur said quietly. 'Just like you did.'

'You mean you killed him for that?'

'It's not that simple.' Arthur took a step back and sat down on a tree stump. 'When I met Zodwa, she connected me with a past I had forgotten. We got married, but I had a problem.' He swallowed and, as a descending moonbeam highlighted his features, I saw the young Arthur who had been so eager to please, a puppy. 'A sex problem. I couldn't do it with a woman . . . how do you say it? I couldn't get it up.' He snickered self-consciously, the way we do when forced to expose our nakedness to strangers. 'I went to medicine men, those rip-off artists, and they cleaned me out. But Zodwa stood by me in all this. She had got some religion, thanks to you and your fucking Passion Play.'

As I opened my mouth to remonstrate with him, hell, Zodwa had got religious long before I met her, Arthur waved the gun at me, a signal for me to shut up. 'I know what you want to say,' he said. 'But after Zodwa left the girls' college, she went wild. Fucked anything with a penis. When I met her, she was in bad shape. But, because I loved her, I thought I would wean her from her ways. It seemed like a good idea for her to go to your brother and get some spiritual sustenance. Only it wasn't spiritual sustenance he was giving her, your brother. When I found one of those vapid love letters she had written to Jonathan, I confronted her. Then she told me about how you had broken her virginity.' He looked me straight in the eye. 'A virgin is a precious thing in the township, did you know that, Bobo?'

I nodded, thinking maybe non-verbal communication would disarm him. What a mess. Arthur, my friend, carrying all this hate through all these decades, what a bloody mess. The man was certifiable. Obliquely, I thought about a successor who would pick up my spear, or, in this instance, my bulging briefcase, and see my assignment through.

'So I brought him here, just like I brought you,' he went on. 'Funny how people get sentimental over dead parents. Shit, the people are dead, man, resting. Look,' he gestured with the gun hand, embracing the spread of the cemetery, 'all those people lying in there, being nutrients and giving real sustenance to the worms. They don't give a flying fuck that you go out there and place fresh flowers and tend to the graves. They're dead. *Finito*, no *manga-manga*.'

Arthur declared that he was a scientist, a geologist. He be-

112

lieved in the immortality of rocks. He knew stones, boulders, pebbles; rock formations, fossils, that was his reality. In the beginning there was rock and in the end there will be rock, rock is the alpha and omega, not human beings. They are transient. In this regard, then, they should stand in awe before greatness, the unchangeable nature of rocks. To this effect, in recognition of their frailty, their insignificance in the face of immutable laws, men mustn't bullshit and fuck other people's wives.

'And you know what happened when I shot him?' Arthur was in full flight now. 'I'll tell you. I got hard. I got hard just imagining it was you I was killing. So,' he asked, brightening up, 'how's that for creative therapy?'

'Arthur . . . ' I began.

'Shut up!' Arthur screamed. 'Just shut the fuck up!'

He stood up from the stump. 'Lie down, Bobo.' He waved the gun to the ground.

When I got to my knees, he leant forward and pressed me against the wet, mossy ground. I smelled the earth and the grass and the stones. I thought of the briefcase in his car, the BMW, the dolphin. *Oh God please help me here in this valley of death with this tormented and twisted man who was once my friend help me because I have sinned Hail Mary three times a day I'll even say mea culpa seven times an hour if you deliver me safe how does a bullet feel when it enters your brain do you hear the bang do you smell anything it would be wrong if I voided myself just imagine being dead in such an unflattering position covered in excrement what rots first the guts or the rest of the body is that why when they do an autopsy they take out the innards first do they smell . . . Prrrr! prrrr! I'm already dead and Satan is talking to Saint Peter negotiating over some dubious souls who gatecrashed a celestial party no it's actually . . . * Arthur talking on his cellular phone. ' . . . yes, he's here. D'you want to talk to him? Hang on, let me pass him on to you.' He extended his hand holding the dark instrument with a luminous display and numbers. 'Very handy, these little Japanese toys.' When I found it awkward to hold it, Arthur pulled me up into a sitting position. I pressed the gadget against my ear.

'Hello?' I said.

'Bobo?' a voice said through the crackle. 'Where the hell have you been?'

'Jonathan. Is that you?'

'Who did you think it was – the Right Reverend James Firth?' Then he laughed at our little inside joke. 'I'm at Arthur's place. Better hurry up. Will be good to see you.' The line went dead.

I looked at Arthur, who had stood up. He took the phone from my hand, pushed in the aerial and stuck it inside his shirt pocket. He looked up at the moon, his own face resembling the heavenly body. Then he looked down at me, offered his arm. I clasped the proffered crutch and got to my feet. The gun was nowhere in sight. Arthur wrinkled his nose.

'I'll loan you a pair of jeans,' he said. 'They might be a bit wide around the waist, but we'll sort it out.'

'Okay,' I said. I found a packet of cigarettes in my jacket pocket, lit one, blew out the smoke and followed Arthur to his chariot parked in the furze, which would take us to his house where my brother waited with his heart overflowing with love and trembling.

The Resurrection of the River Artist

The September heat grew and melted the tar. In the middle distance, it rose and painted unreliable images which danced as if in a fluid swirl. Inside the bus Jomo Khumalo sat and looked through the window at the throngs that had assembled at the bus stop which was some twenty or so metres ahead. The heat inside the bus was punishing; since he was in the back seat, sandwiched between a man smoking a panatella and a worker in overalls whose breath reeked of stale liquor, Jomo felt his gorge rise.

He remembered Bheki, a musician he had known, who had sat wedged in between two coarse men who, by the smell of it, had consumed vast quantities of sorghum beer. As the bus lurched, the men belched and growled their self-praise. *'Yabhodl'inkunzi yomZulu, ukub'umSuthu ngab'uyatshokoza.'* The giant muZulu has burped; if it were a MoSotho, he'd be vomiting. The diesel fumes wafting in through the window and the churning movement of the vehicle must have hastened the attack of nausea in one of the passengers. Since he was nowhere near the window and a young mother on his right was pacifying a squalling baby, he took the path of least resistance and emptied a mix of grainy stomach contents on Bheki's fashionable Sta-Press trousers. Relieved, he caressed the thumbtack-studded head of his knobkerrie, wiped his mouth with his overall sleeve and gave a satisfied burp. Just when Bheki was contemplating action, the man, as if apropos nothing, remarked, *'Kunjalo ne futhi, siyashaya!'* On top of that, we give a thorough hiding.

Beads of perspiration rolled down Jomo's neck into the inside of his collar. He felt the white, starched fabric, ensuring that it retained its stiffness. Even though his skin was being chafed by the edges, he resolved not to loosen it, knowing that a preacher without his collar was as lost as an animal bereft of a lair. He collected his bag and followed the few passengers who were alighting. When he stepped outside, a blast of hot wind hit him, causing him to reel back. An elderly man with grey hair and a limp detached himself from the waiting group and approached Jomo. 'Are you *igosa* Hedges?' he asked. Then he mumbled something about how they had expected a white preacher. Before Jomo could respond, the man took his bag and strode self-importantly to the others. 'He has arrived,' he announced. 'Praise be to the blood of the Lamb!'

The women in the group ululated and did a short, triumphant jig. The villagers all surrounded Jomo, some touching his blue calico robe the way he had seen teenagers mobbing a pop idol. Even though his head swam with confusion, Jomo wished to tell the people that he had come here to pay a debt to his father and was neither a replacement nor the genuine article. He was not yet an *igosa* although he was working hard at it. But he lost his nerve when he saw the expectant expressions on the faces of the welcoming party. Furthermore, admitting that he was not a deacon would have been a final nail in his father's coffin. The leader of the group, Dlamini, pointed at Jomo's shoes. 'We'll take those,' he said.

'What?' Jomo was genuinely surprised

'Your shoes,' Dlamini said simply. 'Your branch must have forgotten to tell you that all the believers walk barefooted here.' Then he tapped a youngster on the shoulder. The boy waited while Jomo unlaced his shoes. He took off his socks and stuffed them inside, suppressing an urge to sniff them first. Absently he wondered if the villagers knew anything about athlete's foot. Well, he told himself as he surrendered his pair of Crockett & Jones, since they don't wear shoes in these climes, it stands to reason that these yokels will conclude that funky feet form part of the arsenal for wrestling with the sophistication of the Evil One in urban areas.

Walking at a brisk trot, the believers sang songs and beat their drums, sweat rolling down their backs and gluing the raiment of faith to their bodies. Although feeling the heat enveloping him like a blanket, Jomo still had time to reflect on the women; they danced and sang, oblivious of the effect their movements might have had on the brethren. I must be a bloody pervert, Jomo thought, feeling a raw sexual tension getting hold of him, remembering other instances where women looked desirable – in the throes of religious passion or when they wept during a funeral. The believers were singing, '*Som'bonga eJolidani Uma siliwela . . .*' a hymn rallying the sinners to submit to the will of the Lord, where they could then be admitted to the community of the faithful and thank the Lord as they crossed the river Jordan.

Jomo, feeling that he would give his eye-teeth for a walk in the river, knew that this trek could prove his undoing. Already he could feel his feet blistering. Concentrating on the houses and shacks and a clutter of rondavels, marvelling at the intricate thatch, pumpkins and miscellaneous odds and ends drying on the corrugated-iron roofs, he was nonetheless aware that the people were looking at him, especially the eager young boy toting his shoes, who gave Jomo a sidelong glance, rating the urban preacher's progress. Jomo knew that if he asked how much longer they had to walk, he would be given the laconic and imprecise village gauge of distances, oh, it's just yonder that hill. And that hill would be fifteen miles away. He was into baptism and believed in total immersion, not immolation.

The tedious rigour of the walk was somewhat leavened by Dlamini, who, in his slow, deliberate delivery, accounted for each member of the congregation. All the people came from Horizon, which was a score of miles from Cato Ridge. All the families had one or two members employed at Faulkner Plywood. 'That is why almost all the houses are built with some form of timber.' Even as he spoke, a breeze from the Vanda hills carried the smell of newly sawn lumber and wood-smoke. It occurred to Jomo that his father's work at Dunlop was somehow connected to his sojourn in Horizon. That and his own uncanny ability to put himself in sticky situations. Here he was, now, in the bundu, away from the few friends he had. An old

117

radio jingle popularising beer played itself in his mind: *Fun, friends and cold Castle, this is the life and this is the beer!* What would his friends say if they saw him now? His erstwhile friends – especially George – would welcome seeing the back of him. He had failed.

Jomo would be the first to admit that his disgrace and failure in the artistic world spurred him to embrace religion. This departure from what he had regarded as his calling caused him little grief, since he understood religious rituals to be part of artistic activity. This ready acceptance was due to the fact that Jomo was no mere preacher. Certainly, he could deliver ringing sermons whose depth of feeling and insights into the dark stirrings of the human heart struck a resonant chord with the most hardened transgressor. But his real strength layin baptising new believers. A self-confessed proponent of total immersion, Jomo had elevated baptism to an art form. He owed all this, in an oblique way, to his father, the chief deacon of the Pentecostal Holiness Church. The deacon had risen from the ranks of the church to the extent that he was invited to address fringe groups at the annual Pentecostal Leaders Convention.

The convention comprised leaders from a myriad of pentecostal churches. Their meetings lay stress on networking, adopting causes and campaigns on human rights, establishing schemes to help people rendered destitute by natural calamities. Since it had originated in England, the PLC had to register as a company for business and tax purposes. Even now, Jomo remembered its notepaper with a logo and a Chelsmford address: *'PLC (plc)'*. Elders of some of the affiliate churches found this vulgar; the younger, more forward-looking clergy thought it a brilliant stroke. 'There's nothing wrong', Pastor John R Hedges, the Director, would justify PLC's activities, 'in raising money in the name of the Lord.'

The British visitor would remark loudly that he was intrigued by the African brethren's attitude to church campaigns. Here they were, conspicuously living high on the hog, driving flashy cars, accompanied by wives whose green robes of sanctity with a white cross sewn on the front and the back to symbolise temperance and thrift but who could still slip in R200 hairstyles and expensive jewellery. But he was impressed with the chief deacon, who didn't have a flashy car. He would learn later that the man just couldn't drive. In this imperfect world, where people were prone to disorders such as dyslexia or night-blindness, the deacon was completely incapable of manipulating a mechanical device.

It was this apprehension of his father's failures which influenced Jomo's attitude to success. His mother, Sibongile, had repeatedly told him that no matter what you did – and no matter how efficiently – there would be someone waiting in the wings to shoot you down. He then had to find a new set of values, where success wouldn't be judged by material assets, or how many people deferred to you. Moreover, even though old Khumalo was a flop, there was no doubt that Sibongile loved him. She regularly stressed that nothing was more important than love. This understanding, of course, did not mean that Khumalo was not an unmitigated disaster.

Even now, people were still talking about how the old man once almost got swallowed up in a retreading mould machine at Dunlop. Workers joked that the cars would by now be rolling down the highways of Durban with tyres impregnated with a special ingredient. After the near-accident, Jomo's father was assigned to a safer section where he merely recorded tyre serial numbers. Not that his numeric skills were anything to crow about, but the deacon had put in nearly thirty years of his life at Dunlop. Even the most mean-spirited of supervisors could not find it in their hearts to let him go. That he had come very close to enriching the quality of rubber also counted in his favour. The deacon was a dedicated man.

It was the end of summer, at the height of the baptismal season when Jomo, who was now dabbling with paints at the Natal Society of Arts in Guildhall Arcade in Durban, went to visit his parents in KwaMashu. Two years earlier he had left his father's house to live with a group of artists and writers in Wills Road, which was as near the city as it could get. The deacon welcomed him in that gruff, distant, affectionate manner fathers reserve for wilful sons. The old man had tried to get his son a job at

Dunlop. Jomo had found the going tough and left the firm before the end of the week without waiting for his wage. Also, he couldn't stand the way the supervisors talked to his father and knew that he had to leave or risk committing homicide. His mother, who worked in a crèche in C Section, was voluble in her happiness. She gathered him in her arms, which smelled of disinfectant, and heated some water for him to take a bath before the evening meal.

As he cleansed himself of the filth of the city, Jomo took in the familiar smells of the bathroom, remembering his life here in the township. The schools he had attended, the friends he had made and the fights he had fought. Looking at the peeling walls, he was reminded of the time his mother caught him with Sonto, the girl who lived next door, and how he had been thrashed. Where was she now, Sonto? Then there was the time when he took up karate, jogging each afternoon after school to the dojo in D Section. The instructors seemed to revel in the knowledge that they could cause pain. There was his short tenure as a counter-hand at Mashiphela's store in H Section, the women he met and the small acts of kindness he did for customers who were short of money. This was what caused Mashiphela to invite him into the office and give him the sack.

It was in his father's eyes as they ate that evening that Jomo saw how the older man had been defeated. In the weak and warm candle-light, where shadows danced across Khumalo's craggy face and created deep furrows like dongas on a parched field, he saw something in his father's eyes – stubbornness? fear? He couldn't tell. But, whatever it was, it spoke of the hard journeys that the man had taken. It had been his dream to knock the kitchen wall down and build another room. 'For visitors. A room for visitors,' he said. But the task hadn't been completed; rubble and a wheelbarrow containing building implements rested in the back, an eloquent testimony to a monumental failure. Jomo's mother looked across the table and her eyes rested on her son's; then she gave an imperceptible shake of the head, an illusion of movement that could have been caused by the shift of the flickering flame. With this, she was imploring her son not to say anything that could hurt.

But that night, Jomo was tired of pandering to his father's delusions. 'How, really,' he asked, 'are you going to finish building? It takes time, labour and, much more importantly, money.'

Khumalo looked up from his plate. 'The money I might not have, not now, anyway,' he said, pointing with a greasy spoon. 'But I thought I had a son who could lend some of his muscle to the task at hand.'

'I can't do it, baba,' Jomo said, feeling something rising up in him. Unaccountably, he felt angry. His father was shifting the blame, accusing him of filial disloyalty. 'I have to paint for an exhibition at the NSA. Whatever little time I have has to go into that.'

'Paint?' Khumalo scoffed. 'What paint? I have seen those things you people do – and they have no connection with reality. People jiving in the township shacks. Guitars and saxophones. Dogs scavenging in garbage bins.' Then he laughed. It was not a nice sound. 'Although I must say you artists seem to be pretty good at painting garbage.'

'Now calm down.' Jomo's mother gave her son an accusing look. 'Why don't you finish your meal, then you can talk about building.'

'Or painting garbage,' Khumalo, sensing victory, put in. 'A while back I saw one of these paintings in a white man's house. At the hotel where Pastor Hedges lives. And I knew that this is not right. Why take our dirty linen to strangers?'

'Because they can fucking well afford it,' Jomo said, 'those bloody strangers you kow-tow to, who make you eat garbage and fill your head with religion.'

'*Jomo!*' His mother was horrified.

Khumalo looked at his son as if from across a great gulf. The silence between the two men became the only living thing in the dining-room. It was a silence which spoke of decades of misunderstanding. 'You know what?' he asked, 'I really feel sorry for you.'

Jomo stood up, almost upsetting the table. He strode to the kitchen where he had left his jacket draped over a chair. He heard his mother's footfalls behind him, the flip-flops on the tiled floor.

'I'm going, ma,' he said. 'Just don't ask me to stay over.'

'You're going to stay,' his mother said, grabbing him by the shoulders and turning him to face her. 'Your father loves you. We love you. In any event, your uncle Mboza heard that you're coming. Him you can argue with.'

'Yes,' Khumalo jeered from the dining-room, 'go ahead and pamper your little black Picasso. Next time he'll be painting life-sized turds that have a realistic smell.'

Jomo rolled up his eyes and threw his hands in the air. He wanted to get back and confront his father and tell him that Picasso, for all his inventiveness, had been influenced by African art. But he knew that his father would just eviscerate him with a word. Such knowledge was, in any event, beneath him. Jomo's mother held him with her eyes.

'Don't say a word.' She went to a cupboard and retrieved a half-empty bottle of scotch whisky. Without a word she poured him a measure in a tumbler.

Mboza arrived just then, lugging a heavy knapsack. He was a short, thickset man with a beer belly and a booming laugh. Everything about him spoke of his physical nature. Jomo loved him, but tried always to maintain a distance, for the simple reason that, like most big men, Mboza didn't really know his own strength. That and his proclivity for slapping you hard on the shoulder when amused. It was not difficult to see how much havoc he could wreak in a moment of anger.

Having got rid of the load on the table, Mboza proceeded to embrace his sister. Jomo stood looking on, marvelling at the way his mother's face changed as she giggled, saying, '*Suka lapha, wena* Mboza – get away,' and Mboza looking like a big tomcat, his eyes riveted to the bottle. Then he turned and came to wrestle with Jomo, pinning him down, calling him to surrender. 'Tell me now you want a give-up.'

'Give-up, give-up,' Jomo said, feeling that his arm would break. When he had got to his feet, he stroked his arm. 'Mboza,' he said, 'you almost broke my arm, you big bastard. Why don't you use your mugging skills where they are most needed?'

'Where's that?'

'In the criminal fraternity,' Jomo said. 'I know of one visiting pastor from England who could redeem us from this poverty which is causing my father to be so crazy.'

'I heard that!' Khumalo said from the dining-room. 'And I can tell there's drinking going on there . . .'

Mboza laughed, showing a row of uneven teeth. As he helped himself to the whisky, he said: 'I might just need some help from that quarter. I'm in deep shit.'

'What has happened this time?' Jomo's mother asked.

Mboza pulled back a chair and straddled it. Reaching into his knapsack, his hand came out with an assortment of twigs, pieces of bark and what seemed like wood shavings. Suddenly the kitchen was filled with a wild, oily odour. Jomo's mother sniffed disapprovingly. 'Don't put those things on my kitchen table.'

'*Hawu*, Sibongile,' Mboza said, 'why do you believers pretend you know nothing about healing herbs?' He looked up at her. 'My father was a herbalist and all of us were weaned on traditional medicine, so what's the bleeding about?'

'Your brother-in-law will have a fit that you brought *muthi* into his house.' Jomo's mother crossed her arms against her breast. 'You know how he is.'

'I've got something that can cure him, too,' Mboza said carelessly. Placing his cache of herbs on an old issue of *Ilanga Lase Natal*, he directed himself to Jomo. '*Mshana*,' he said, isolating a cutting, 'this is *umelemele*. Got it in Rhodesia.'

'Zimbabwe,' Jomo corrected him.

'Okay, Zimbabwe,' Mboza said. 'I had to fix up a guy at work, one of the excuse-me types, who has a problem with . . .' he glanced at his sister, ' . . . his equipment, you know?'

'I don't think I want to hear this,' Jomo's mother said, but she didn't move.

'What was the problem?' Jomo asked, settling down and taking a sip of his drink. 'You mean he couldn't get it up.'

'Worse,' Mboza said, 'he doesn't have anything to get up. He's built like a boy. He has been complaining that he thinks his wife is fooling around on account of that.'

'Jesus,' Sibongile said, suppressing a giggle. 'What a world!'

''Strue's God,' Mboza explained, 'it's just like this . . . ' extending his small finger. 'So I got him *umelemele* and told him to strap it to his thing. Because of its size I advised him to use Sellotape. Then I gave him another cutting and instructed him to plant it in a secret place in the garden.' He paused and pointed at his empty glass. 'Pour me another drink, will you, Bongi?'

Jomo watched his mother pouring out the drinks. He slapped at his neck when a mosquito buzzed him, whining against his ear. Mboza took a sip.

'Two weeks later I asked him how's it going,' he said, 'and he assured me that there were some promising developments. Then this morning, he breezes in like the demons are after him and finds me drinking my tea. I ask him what's the matter and he says that he planted the cutting somewhere in the middle of the garden. When he came back from work his wife had lev-elled the whole thing and workmen were busy laying concrete there.'

'Jesus,' Sibongile said again. 'What happened?'

'I made a mistake and laughed. That's when he hit the roof, accusing me of ridiculing him. I said, Hey, I'm not your wife, I didn't put cement over your damn cutting . . . ' Mboza shook his head. 'His problem is that he thinks I'll tell the other men and he'll be the laughing-stock. What he doesn't know is that the other guys know everything already. So, now he says he'll hire some killers who'll do one thing with me.' He sighed. 'There's just no gratitude in this world, *Mshana*. Try and help someone, then you become public enemy number one.'

Jomo reassured his uncle that the man would one day come to his senses and make peace with him. Later that evening, they went to a shebeen at D Section and drank until the small hours. They returned to the house and slept.

In the morning, a slightly hungover Jomo took the train to Berea Road and proceeded to the NSA studios to hustle some money for materials and palliatives for the mynah birds that were get-ting out of hand in his head. As luck would have it, the first person he met was Zelda Retamane, the formidable curator. She was a complex woman of indeterminate age and ambiguous sexuality. For someone who had studied – and taught – art in

institutions at home and abroad, she was pretty staid about colour, always in brown, beige or sepia. Her brown hair was always tightly encased in a scarf. One of the wise guys from
Lamontville, George, had earned her undying enmity by de-
claring that her name was an anagram for 'lazed man-eater';
the final nail in his own coffin was the rumour he had spread
that, beneath the wig, Zelda was actually as bald as an egg. She
was not the type to brood when she hated someone, she did
something about it. It was common knowledge that George
would never exhibit with NSA despite the fact that he was the
most gifted of the crop. But George was not worried about
being blacklisted; he always arrived in disguise to these events
from which he was banned. Then he would taunt her over the
phone. 'Do you remember the Malawian envoy you spent the
whole evening charming?' he would ask. 'Well, that was me,
you wretched cow.'

But – at the same time – Zelda did push the frontiers for black
artists. She had earned the ire of all-white establishments who
wanted to take on black artists on their own terms. Many promising people had given up trying, especially since the white
patrons had arrogated the right to advise black artists on subject matter. Depicting white people or Europeans was, for instance, out of the question. The artists were enjoined to draw
idyllic curio-like images of tribal scenes. Zelda wrote long po-
lemics against this kind of artistic neo-colonialism. In this way,
then, a steady stream of black artists found a home in her studios.

This morning, though, she was in a foul mood. She had been
trying to appropriate the works of an erratic South African exile painter who was single-mindedly killing himself via cocaine
and alcohol in London. Many exiles had come back after the
release of Nelson Mandela and the legalisation of once-banned
political movements. But Ethan Bundu was clear that he had
made London his home. He was scared of returning to South
Africa for the simple reason that he was broke. And his home
country was reputed to take a dim view of failures. The irony
was that his works were in catalogues and galleries world-wide,
but since he had a habit to support, he had flogged his pieces

for a song, just enough change for a hit. Collectors were refusing to grant Zelda the rights for what would have become one of the definitive exhibitions in South Africa. 'What's worse', she wailed, 'is that we could collect a lot of money for Ethan. Get him a nice place to detox in Cape Town.'

'Maybe', Jomo suggested helpfully, the mynahs going *wah–wah! woh–woh!* in his head, 'you should get someone from the CCB to kidnap him.'

Zelda gave him a long look while massaging her temples with her forefingers. It was then that Jomo realised that she had beautiful brown eyes. 'You're drunk again,' Zelda said. 'So early in the morning and you're already stinking up the place. Why don't you pull yourself together?'

Jomo knew that any talk of money might prove suicidal. Then the birds gave him an idea. 'Why don't you mount an exhibition without Ethan. Get one of his relatives to stand in for him? There's nothing unethical about that.'

'Problem is we've failed completely to trace any living relative,' Zelda lamented. 'What's even more galling is that the only pictures we have of him were taken more than twenty years ago . . . ' Her voice trailed off. 'Come with me,' she commanded.

He followed her down the corridor to the steel door leading to the fire escape. After much heaving, Zelda got the door open. From where he stood, Jomo could see the roofs of buildings, pigeons roosting in their perches. A blast of cool morning wind hit them at that altitude, causing Zelda's skirts to shoot up as in a parody of Marilyn Monroe's famous pose. Then they went up a flight of steel stairs and entered a door marked *PRIVATE.* Inside it was dark until Zelda switched on the lights. It was a darkroom where the trays were still full of stale developer and fixer solutions. Zelda climbed on a stool and reached the top of a cupboard. She returned with a folder which she handed to Jomo. Then she switched off the lights and they went back to the studio.

Separating a selection of glossy black-and-white prints from the pile in the folder, she handed them one by one to Jomo. The face which stared back at him belonged to a medium-height black man with intense, brooding eyes, a broad forehead, lips turned downwards as if the owner was debating whether to smile or scowl, a moustache and a well-kept beard. As she passed the pictures on to Jomo, Zelda did not take her eyes off him.

'What do you think?' she asked. She seemed barely able to contain her excitement.

'Looks okay to me,' Jomo said, not knowing what the hell she expected him to think.

'Looks a lot like you,' she said, 'wouldn't you say?'

'To white people, maybe.'

A cloud of irritation flashed across Zelda's face. 'I'm an artist, Jomo, my dear,' she said. 'And I have done a study of faces. Negroid, Caucasoid, Mongoloid – you name it, I've done it. I'm not one of your run-of-the-mill whiteys for whom all blacks look the same. This man,' she went on, tapping the photograph with a forefinger, 'you're a dead ringer for him.'

'I wouldn't know,' Jomo said, suddenly feeling that he was being swamped in something he wished to avoid. 'I haven't looked in the mirror in the longest time.'

'Take my word for it.' She gave him one of her strange looks again. 'Do you have a passport?'

'No.'

'We'll organise you one.' Then she pulled him to her and gave him a kiss full on the lips. 'You lovely drunk, you, you've made my day.'

Then she gave him fifty rands and told him where to go to apply for a passport. She would supply the references. 'You can cure the hangover with the change,' she said from the top of the stairs. 'You've earned it.'

The day was damp and grey when, two weeks later, Jomo and Zelda walked out of Heathrow Airport's Terminal 4 to lug their bags to the Underground. The flight had been unmemorable simply because the two had anaesthetized themselves to the journey with whiskys and gins-and-tonics. It seemed to Jomo, as he balanced on the strap in the moving train, that he was doomed to experience life through an alcoholic haze. He had decided against taking a seat, knowing that the rocking motion of the train would lull him to sleep.

Jomo was amazed, after they had negotiated their way out of the confusion of King's Cross Station, how the streets of London teemed with black people. He gawped at women in short skirts and fishnet stockings who plied their trade openly, and at this early hour. Derelicts sat propped against the plate glass of W H Smith's, sipping Thunderbird wine and Holstein lager. Across the street young blacks, some sporting dreadlocks, and whites, all dressed in black, casually stopped people, obviously peddling something, furtively slinking into the kebab-and-chips joint when a bobby appeared. The cops themselves walked with an easy gait, something about their attitude communicating their familiarity with sleaze. The newspaper and tobacco kiosks exhibited their stock of glossy magazines where naked women pouted as their posed in parodies of seduction and ecstasy. The eyes of the people stepping out of the deep Underground cavern said it all: *We are so lonely.*

This loneliness was in the eyes of the mid-morning drinkers in the pubs. Zelda, reading from a piece of paper, directed a cab driver to an address in Islington. As they sat in the back, the meter clicking and flashing like a curse, Jomo looked out of the window at the traffic which belched up Pentonville Road, past the reservoir which rose, green like baize topping a snooker table; they turned into Penton Street, and the driver, hearing that they were from South Africa, pointed out the ANC offices. Then they passed the Chapel Market where buyers, mainly housewives and single mothers, browsed, picking at fabrics from the stalls, the vendors shouting in accented tones.

Ethan Bundu lived on the second floor of a maisonette on Cross Street. The flat overlooked Picture Frames, an establishment catering to the needs of artists. Zelda told the driver to wait while she rang the bell. She disappeared inside a hallway and was gone for a few minutes. She came back and told the cabby to take them to The Slug & Lettuce, a public house on Upper Street. Cinema buffs were already lined up outside The Screen on the Green, where Martin Scorsese's *Goodfellas* was showing. As they left the taxi, Jomo could hear strains of cool jazz coming out of Tower Records, a shop separated from the film theatre by a narrow lane. Having crossed the street, Jomo and Zelda entered the pub. There were a few serious drinkers already, yuppie and city types going to seed. Ethan sat in a corner alone, drinking half-and-halves, a double scotch whisky chased quickly down with a half-pint of lager. Although in need of a drink himself, Jomo found the older man's choice a little grim.

Ethan had not so much aged as surrendered to a force inside him which was working assiduously towards his dissolution. He was not a big man, but the bony fingers wrapped around the glass, and the grey, balding head supporting a thin neck spoke of an epidermal struggle to contain a skeleton that was impatient to emerge. Only his eyes, troubled and infinitely sad, connected him to the memory Jomo had of him. Jomo had once seen pictures of the Ethiopian leader, Haile Selassie, taken hours before his execution. Ethan could as well have been wearing the deposed emperor's death mask.

Ethan looked up from his drink. 'You've come to see me?' he asked, unsurprised. Without waiting for their answer he waved a hand in the general direction of the chairs. 'Do sit down.' His voice was deep and hoarse.

'I hope we're not troubling you,' Zelda said, seeming quite uncomfortable as she edged her slight frame into the booth. 'This is Jomo.'

'My successor,' Ethan said. He smiled; his sallow skin looked like his teeth. 'I won't say I'm pleased to see you. I don't have time for those niceties. But I am relieved.'

'Relieved?' Zelda was puzzled.

'Yes. It's about time.'

Someone, somewhere in the smoky, cavernous bar fed a tape to a stereo. There was a whirr and a click, then soft strains of strings followed by a percussive, insistent bass. Then Marvin Gaye wailed, singing a sad song, making a statement which had been repeated so many times that it had become everyone's automatic truth.

'*Ooh, I heard it through the grapevine . . .*' and Jomo wondered whether Ethan, who must have been freezing in his open-necked shirt and lightweight grey suit and thin shoes, understood the meaning of the words. The singer had also known exile, and he

129

had also been troubled, and he had gone back home to die.

'Whenever South Africans approach me,' Ethan said, 'I'm always convinced that they want something out of me. They see me as a tortured genius that needs redemption.' He paused and lit a cigarette. 'But it never occurs to them how much *they* need help. Especially people in the arts, they're really fucked up.'

'What do you mean?' Jomo asked.

'I've never met people who are so utterly bereft of graciousness,' Ethan said. 'There were many of us here, artists, musicians, poets, writers. We were a community, perhaps we were bonded together by our exile. But beneath this bonding was such jealousy as you've never known. Whenever one of us made it somehow, we partied. But as the liquor ran and the tongues loosened, you heard the venom, people cutting each other up, running each other down.'

He swallowed something that must have tasted very bitter. 'For us, for me,' he went on, 'I discovered the horror of life, and this discovery was thanks to curators and gallery owners. They were all invariably white and they treated black artists with contempt. Sure, they organised us gigs, seeing that we couldn't enter that world of exhibitions and cheese-and-wine parties under our own steam. But still they exploited us, not financially; that is a given. They exploited us through a single-minded withdrawal of affection. When they talked about us to their genteel friends in Hampstead, they would say, Sure, Ethan is gifted, but he is nothing but a drunk. This happened with me when I was seven months on the wagon. When told about this, I said, Fuck it. Then I started hitting the bottle again.' As if to punctuate the last statement, he leaned forward and emptied his glass. After taking a sip from his lager, he gave a deep sigh.

'We got together, the brothers and sisters,' he said, 'and we talked about this. We said, we have to survive. Some of us – those who didn't believe what the white world was saying about them – somehow made it across the water. But we're not made from the same mould. With some of us, the contempt stung and rendered us impotent. We looked at our creations, *knew* we were good, but couldn't function until the curators had stamped that knowledge with their approval.'

Zelda got to her feet. Jomo was scared that she was going to walk out on them. 'Where are you going?'

'To get a drink,' Zelda said. 'I see you're having whisky and lager,' she addressed Ethan. 'Are you having another?'

'Of course,' Ethan said with a small smile. 'I knew when you came in through that door that this was a lady after my own heart.'

'Jomo?'

'I'll have whatever he's having.' Jomo suddenly felt reckless.

Jomo did not know how long they had stayed in the bar until the lunch-time crowd streamed in. By this time, Ethan had told them that he knew they had come for his work – and he would give it to them. 'But you have to get us a taxi,' he said, 'because I have no intention of taking the Tube to Camden.'

'That's in order,' Zelda said, relieved. She couldn't bring herself to meet Jomo's eyes. He wondered what had happened to her; she should have whooped for joy, seeing that her job was almost done, and it hadn't been so difficult. He knew, however, that, whatever people said, it took a thoroughly liberated white person to accept criticism from black people. The country was in turmoil. South Africa was now prefaced with the fashionable adjective 'New'. But the reality was that the sons and daughters of the masters of the land still ruled the roost. The struggle had come and gone; whatever blood had been shed, whites had not bled. Their transition from the comfortable state apartheid had bequeathed them to the much-vaunted new dispensation had been painless. This absence of pain meant a corresponding, albeit unspoken and subliminal, acceptance of – and sometimes a yearning for – that idyllic state when the world had been created in their collective image.

Later, as they rode in the taxi, Jomo reflected on the arrogance of power. He remembered hearing that, after the elections, businessmen had boasted that, now that the blacks had political power, they, the leaders of business and industry, would concentrate on their God-given task of controlling the economy.

'What are you thinking, Zelda?' Ethan broke the silence in the cab.

'Nothing,' Zelda said in a small voice. 'Except that what my people have done is so wrong.'

'Don't worry,' Ethan put in, stroking her shoulder. 'When you get back home, all this will seem like a bad dream, and, as John Major would say, it will be back to basics.'

'That's unfair. I'm not a racist.'

'Don't worry about it. Time will tell.'

As they drove along Pratt, he showed them the road, Mandela Street, which led to the offices of the Anti-Apartheid Movement. Then, nearer the tube station, the new Jazz Café. 'Two nights ago Baaba Maal was performing here. He brought the house down.'

The taxi dropped them off at the bridge leading to Camden Lock. Tourists and natives milled around the stalls. Ethan led them past Dingwalls, another jazz joint, up a flight of rickety stairs until he bade them wait for him while he entered a stall where exotic chocolates were on display. Down below, on ground level, a book stall was doing a brisk trade. Zelda ducked under an awning and went into a shop selling masks and vases of intricate designs. Soon enough, Ethan came back holding a heavy black leather portfolio.

'Let's go,' he said.

They followed him down the stairs to the path leading to the canal. He politely refused Jomo's offer to help carry the bag. They negotiated their way past shoppers and children who carried balloons sporting names of famous departmental stores. On their left, the hull of a polished boat blocked their view of the other side.

'You say your father is a preacher?' Ethan said as they went under the bridge. 'Did he teach you anything?'

Jomo replied that Khumalo was disappointed with him. But, when young, he had been his father's constant companion. 'I even took up swimming,' he confessed, 'in case I was ever called on to baptise people. Then I studied the Bible, but for me it was to confront Jehovah's Witnesses. It became so bad that I would actually accost them on the streets just so I could engage them. I guess I must have been the first fourteen-year-old kid that was *avoided* by Jehovah's Witnesses.'

'Well,' Ethan said, handing the bag to Zelda, 'this is my lucky day.'

'What do you mean?' Jomo asked.

'I know I'm going to die,' Ethan said. 'It's just a matter of time. But, as things stand here, no minister can baptise a drunk like me.'

It took Jomo a while before the penny dropped. 'You mean you want *me* to baptise *you*?'

Ethan nodded. 'That's right. Surely,' he said, 'after what I've given you, you can't refuse.'

'I can refuse. No.'

'Well,' Ethan said, reaching for the portfolio, 'then we can part company. It was nice knowing you.'

'*Jomo!*' Zelda's voice cut like a whiplash through the air. 'What do you think you're doing?'

'He wants me to baptise him. That's crazy.'

'Then you'll fucking baptise him,' Zelda said. Her face was red, the eyes had turned from brown to grey. She started pushing Jomo towards the edge of the concrete path. Jomo resisted the temptation to grab her *and* Ethan and his bloody portfolio and push them into the drink.

'Why can't you wait until we get to a decent river?' Jomo asked Ethan. 'Or come back with us to Africa. There are rivers there.'

'Stop with the rhapsodies about the rivers of Africa, Jomo. Fucking baptise the man!'

Jomo looked at her for what seemed a very long time. Slowly, he started taking off his jacket, to be followed by his shoes. Remembering that he was wearing polka-dot boxer shorts, he decided to keep his pants on. A slight drizzle was now falling, cold, causing him to shiver. 'Come,' he said to Ethan, 'let's go in.' He hoped that the canal was not deep.

As the two men jumped into the canal, shoppers and tourists looked on, shaking their heads. One of the derelicts gaped, showing toothless gums. 'Hey, Phil,' he shouted, nudging his partner, 'take a look what the niggers is doing.'

The shock of the cold water made Jomo gasp. Then he was under the surface, tasting the oil and something that was as vile as Mboza's potions. The water was red, like the first rays of the sun at dawn. As he reached out, flailing, he got hold of Ethan's jacket. *He's going to drown, dear God, and we'll be accused of murder!* Panic seized him as he surfaced, taking great gulps of air into his lungs. Then he pulled Ethan up and held his thin frame against himself. It felt as if he were gathering a bunch of kindling, so thin was the man. Baptism, he asked himself, how did his father do it? What did he say?

Then the words cascaded out of his mouth, unbidden, like a desperate prayer before an execution. 'Dear Father,' he said, 'accept this sinner, Ethan Bundu, who has now confessed his sins and renounced the world.' Shoving Ethan's head under the water, he heard from a distance someone screaming. As he brought Ethan up again, the screaming became louder and more desperate. *Down.* This time he also followed the artist. *Up!* They broke the water. 'Ethan Bundu,' he said, dunking him for the last time, 'you are now a new man and you have been cleansed of your sins. In the name of the Father and the Son and the Holy Ghost. Welcome to the royal fellowship of the sanctified.'

Later, in the taxi back to The Slug & Lettuce, Ethan, who was shivering uncontrollably, smiled wordlessly, now and then shaking his head as if he had witnessed a miracle. 'Thank you, bro,' he said. 'Thank you.'

'Amen,' Zelda said. 'Now we are going to hit the town.'

Jomo didn't see Zelda for a month after their return home. He heard on the grapevine that she was busy preparing for an exhibition. Not seeing her didn't bother him, except when the money she had given him ran out. George, whenever he bumped into his friend, interrogated him on what had transpired in London, but Jomo had been sworn to secrecy. A rumour started flying around that the lazed man-eater had finally got her claws into Jomo. He was quick to rebut that, saying that, although he wasn't without unusual appetites, Zelda was certainly not on his menu.

He had put her and their trip out of his mind when she called him and gave him the date of the exhibition. She had worked non-stop organising the venue and caterers for the obligatory cocktail party, doing the guest list and sending out invitations. George, of course, was not on the list; Zelda, knowing of her enemy's trickiness with disguises, instructed the security people to check out with her if they saw 'anyone who looks like a surreal killer'. And, on this occasion, she stood at the entrance, ensuring that no local artist gate-crashed the opening. The invitations were for the select few, art collectors and the good and the great of the land. When Jomo was ushered into the gallery, and when he saw a blown-up black-and-white photograph of himself with the legend, *Ethan Bundu*, underneath, he experienced a strange, almost surreal sense of being there in the room and, at the same time, of being underwater in a dirty Camden Lock canal. Zelda was beside him, a proprietary hand on his arm.

'What do you think?' she asked.

'Hell, I don't know.' Jomo's eyes panned across the pen-and-ink prints, woodcuts, etchings and five or six oil pastels. The urban and rural landscapes and figures that seemed to leap out of the canvases were done with such strong lines it was difficult to associate them with the frail man Jomo had met. It was as if Ethan had been aware of his infirmity, and this was his testament, an affirmation of his quest for life. The common feature uniting the work was the theme of water; a jug silhouetted against a window while, in the background, a bulldozer razes a shack. Children racing across a flooded street. Water cascading down a small rapids under which a woman with prominent breasts bathes.

He knew then that Ethan Bundu was a man who was clear about his own priorities. He was grossly misunderstood by critics who wished to fit him within a pigeon-hole, define him and thereafter destroy him. Somewhere in the darkroom where Jomo had seen Ethan's picture, there were old interviews with the newspapers, where Ethan had been asked about socially responsive art. Even now, as he stood there, Jomo could hear the sneer in the journalist's tone, dripping with venom, merely because the interviewer had his own idea of what art should be. Ethan had answered him simply, and told him of the artists in Europe who had joined the war against Fascism. Ethan reminded the man of women such as Käthe Kollwitz, Eva Hesse, of Paula Modersohn-Becker. Some of these women's work had been dismissed as propaganda. 'What is propaganda?' Ethan had asked. 'For me, it is work devoted to some creed or doctrine. And, as a South African, this work would be meaningless if I didn't somehow espouse a doctrine that would do away with death.' It was clear, from these pronouncements, that Ethan would not last in the country. After being detained repeatedly, he applied for an exit permit. The regime of the day granted him a one-way exit out of his country.

Jomo had not, until he saw Ethan in London, bothered to understand the tensions and anxieties which attended exile. For the most part, people who had left were cowards, rats abandoning a sinking ship. Then there were stories which the regime's media were quick enough to publicise, that exiles were living it up in the fleshpots of European capitals, marrying white women and forgetting about the struggle back home. He had heard, for instance, of the mansion which Oliver Tambo was supposed to have occupied. During their sojourn in London, he asked Zelda to take them to Muswell Hill, to satisfy his eyes. What he saw was . . . just a house. Oliver Tambo was long gone and the house was now rented out to the Zambian High Commission. There was no sign of the mansion. We have been weaned on lies, he thought. Perhaps, with all the hidden things coming to light now, we shall be a whole and saner people. The truth will have to set us free.

When his eyes rested on the invited guests, most of them resplendent in evening dress, he suddenly doubted whether he wanted to go along with this deception. 'Did we really have to do it this way?' he asked. 'I mean, exhibitions have been held for an absent artist before . . . ?'

'What you don't realise', Zelda said, using the same tone she had used at the canal, 'is that people want to see the creator, in flesh and blood. The real McCoy.'

'But . . . ?'

'But nothing!' Zelda snapped. 'Just get yourself a glass of wine, mingle and look like a tortured artist.' She patted him on the back, absently, the way people do when enjoying a pedigreed dog. 'You *are* a tortured artist, after all, aren't you?'

Jomo stood staring at her, stumped for a smart retort. Before he could say anything, she had sashayed away to greet more notables and keep an eye out for the Lamontville Pimpernel. He got himself a glass of wine and speared a sausage with a toothpick. Around him, the patrons were examining the prints, now and then turning to give him those nervous toothpaste grins business people reserve for artists. Some shook his hand and congratulated him on a brilliant exhibition. And: 'We must get together for a drink some time.' In no time Jomo was holding about a dozen business cards.

Zelda, glass in hand, announced that the artist would speak. The murmurs stopped and all eyes turned to Jomo. She had given him a prepared text; he searched in his pockets, feeling like a man from whom a policeman was demanding a pass, and couldn't find it. The eyes of the patrons seemed to melt, recede and blaze as if they were being focused upon with a zoom lens. His mouth felt as if he had swallowed sawdust and he felt his knees start to buckle. I'm not going to disgrace myself, he said to himself. I'm going to say my piece. To hell with this.

Just then the door opened, letting in a young woman in a flowing golden kaftan and a matching head-dress, and feet encased in leather sandals; she was pursued in earnest by security guards who couldn't keep up with her pace. Tall and sinewy, she was one of those people who immediately stand out in a crowd, as graceful in her movements as a dancer, or a female panther. Her eyes swivelled to the giant photograph which had Ethan Bundu's name under it. Her face clouded and contorted in rage and disgust. Looking at the prints and the accompanying text, she curled her lips and seemed to have been on the point of saying something when she controlled herself and looked straight at Jomo.

Jomo looked at her eyes, remembering them from somewhere. Just as the penny dropped, Ethan came in, walking slowly, looking around him as if unaware of others. Zelda, her white face as pale as a sheet, stepped towards him as the young woman went forward to confront Jomo.

'Have you people no shame?' she demanded. 'What did you

think you were doing?'

Jomo found that his tongue had attached itself to the roof of his mouth. But, strangely, this discovery that Ethan had a daughter – for, he knew, she must have been the daughter: those eyes! – left him so relieved that he feared he would fall. He heard as if from a great distance, Ethan speaking in measured tones, saying that, when he was baptised, at that moment when he was under water, he saw that he wanted to live. 'I remembered that I had left my people back home,' he said. 'I knew I had a daughter somewhere – and that I wanted to claim her.'

'But we agreed . . . ?' Zelda said lamely. Around them, the patrons looked on with puzzled expressions. 'You've fucked up my show but royally,' she continued. Through the wall of bodies, Jomo saw Ethan's face, fuller now as if he had been to a health farm, the skin clearer and the grey hair combed back. There was such a deep tenderness in his eyes that Jomo was forced to look away.

'Look,' he said to the artist's daughter, 'don't ask me anything.' He pointed at Zelda. 'You see that woman talking to your father? Go and speak to her. Me, I'm out of here.'

As he walked out of the gallery, he heard Zelda shouting at him, threatening him, telling him that he was finished. It didn't need her to tell him that. It was written on the surface of the water.

He then trudged the streets of the city looking for work or, according to his father, real work. In this search, he realised something he had known but had shifted to the farthest recesses of his mind: being unemployed in the city was a hideous state to be in. Sometimes, Mboza took Jomo with him and he worked as a casual labourer, getting paid by the day. Most of the work he found himself doing was soulless and mind-numbing. But the men who carried things and acted as white supervisors' 'spanner-boys' went on, day in and day out, scrubbing, polishing, hoeing and never complaining.

The newspapers were curiously silent about Zelda's artistic caper, convincing Jomo that, in her preparation for the exhibition, some money must have exchanged hands. Whenever he was in town, he would look at the posters around the City Hall. Ethan Bundu exhibiting at the University of Natal. Ethan Bundu in a one-man exhibition at the Durban Playhouse. He was slowly moving from painting and drawing to sculpture. Ethan Bundu's star was rising, he was, as they said in these parts, the flavour of the month. Jomo, remembering his words at The Slug & Lettuce, wished him well, knowing how brittle he was and how hard the people in the art world were. He wondered what had happened to his daughter, feeling an insupportable urge to meet her, if only for an instant. He knew, though, that this was, as usual, a dream.

And then it happened. Mboza dropped in one Sunday morning and told him that he was needed at his father's house. Thinking that something tragic had happened, Jomo dressed quickly and got into his uncle's battered borrowed *bakkie* – 'Mshana, you don't expect me to ride trains on a Sunday, do you?' – and they were in the township three-quarters of an hour later.

Jomo found his parents looking grave, the old man in a dark suit, Sibongile in a nightgown. He wondered why they were not in church, a Sunday ritual they followed unfailingly. He knew that it had to be something much nearer to an injunction from God which could make them break this weekly habit. Khumalo soon apprised his son of what was happening. He had been suspended from the church by Pastor Hedges. He had conducted a baptism in Umngeni River and one of the women had been swept away by the water. It was a stroke of pure luck that her robes had snagged on the reeds and she could be rescued. This incident had riled Hedges, who felt that it was a sign from above that Khumalo was not equipped to execute this task, a kind of celestial vote of no-confidence.

'So,' Jomo asked after his mother had given him a cup of tea, 'what's the big deal?'

Khumalo glared at his son and then looked at his wife as if saying, Well, what did you expect from the turd-illustrator?

'Speak to your son, MaZondi,' Khumalo said and disappeared somewhere in the house.

'Jomo,' Sibongile said, 'this thing has hurt your father. What's even worse is that the other deacons, *black people like him*, they dredged up all the terrible stuff about your father. One time he couldn't exorcise the evil spirits out of a young woman, and it is supposed to be his fault. But the woman was pregnant, and do you think they warned your father? Of course they didn't. They wanted to see him fail.' She let this sink in. 'Do you know how difficult it is to exorcise the evil spirits out of someone who's pregnant?' She shook her head at this herculean task. 'It's impossible.'

'So,' Jomo asked, 'what do you want me to do?'

'I don't know,' Sibongile wailed. 'But something must be done, else all of us will go crazy.' She paused. 'Your father is beginning to say wild things, especially at night. How he is not worthy of the grace of the Lord, that a sign has been given. It's like living with . . . a stranger. What's more, your father was supposed to go to baptise some people in Horizon, and I don't think Hedges will give it to him. And your father was looking forward to doing it.'

'But', Jomo said, 'this Hedges. He's not even from around here. Why doesn't he go back to England and call the shots there?' He wondered why the mere mention of the man's name irritated him so much.

'Well,' Sibongile said, expelling a great gust of air from her lungs, 'he's here and he's the bossman. Whatever he says goes.'

A germ of an idea was developing in Jomo's mind. 'We'll see.' He signalled to his uncle. 'Let's go.'

'Later, Bongi,' Mboza said to his sister.

'Whatever you do,' Jomo's mother said as she watched them getting into the van, 'please be careful.'

Later, at Wills Road, Jomo made a phone call.

'Hi, it's me,' he said.

'Jomo? You've got a nerve calling me —'

'Zelda? I need a favour.'

'You need a favour – from me? It's a fucking hangman you need.'

'Seriously. To speak the truth, you owe me one.'

'Yeah? How's that?

'Because I retreated. I never squawked a word and I'm out of your life.'

'And if I do you this one favour you promise to disappear for ever?'

'Yes.'

There was a long silence, then the receiver crackled into life again. 'What is it that you want?' Jomo told her. When he finished he was again rewarded with silence, and then Zelda started laughing, and the laughter bubbled to become a shriek. 'You're crazy, do you know that?'

'I know,' Jomo said. 'Meet me at the foyer of The Palace at three o'clock.' Then, on putting the phone down, he turned to his uncle, who was reading the racing section of the *Sunday Tribune*. 'Mboza, do you still have all your stuff with you?'

'It's all in the bag,' Mboza said, patting his knapsack. Jomo had an impression that he went to bed with the sack beside him. Must get in the sack with the sack. The absurdity of the thought made him smile, but Mboza, who was pencilling off eternally elusive sure winners, didn't notice. It must be his security blanket, Jomo thought, like Whatsisname, that kid with the funny hair in the Peanuts comic strip.

When Jomo and Mboza entered the foyer of The Palace Hotel, Jomo was struck by the cosiness inside, as if the establishment had been built with a family on a winter afternoon in mind. But what was almost intimidating, until Jomo had to convince himself that he was in the New South Africa, was the number of white people. Men, women and children, dressed casually and exchanging frosty greetings, came in or out, asking the receptionists for messages. They looked at Jomo and Mboza with eyes that didn't register their presence; when Jomo's eyes met those of the women, the latter quickly looked away, their faces twiching, momentarily, as if they had seen something unwholesome. A few Africans in business suits or West African *agbadas* conversed in French; the attitude of the whites to these exotic visitors was markedly different. There were Africans and Africans.

It had always been borne in on Jomo that the white section of society might as well have been born to opulence and comfort. They were born into shiny motor cars, houses with fireplaces, horses and rambling gardens, refrigerators and humming elevators; they took this kind of living in their stride – for granted, even – the way a fish would not need an interlocutor to tell it that water was its habitat. The blacks in livery looked uncomfortable whenever they laid eyes on other blacks who were not in the hotel employ. This puzzled him too.

Zelda sat in one of the low hotel chairs, sipping a coke and smoking a cigarette. Today she had on dark glasses, a cheesecloth shirt and a light-blue skirt which hiked up her legs when she leant forward to tap the ash into an ashtray. On her side lay a raffia bag in which she placed her cigarette pack when she saw them enter. Then she shifted to make room for the men. Thinking that they weren't seeing her, she stuck two fingers between her lips and released a piercing whistle. The hotel customers turned to look at her with disapprobation, as if concluding that the Western sun must have finally set when even white women were adopting common African ways. Removing her glasses, Zelda waved at Jomo. The two men joined her. Quickly, Jomo did the introductions. 'Have you got the stuff ready?' he asked Mboza.

Mboza rummaged into his bag and took out a small, flat snuff tin. He opened it and asked them to dab their nostrils with the balm. That done, Jomo asked Zelda to direct them to Pastor John R Hedges's room. Zelda had followed Hedges earlier in the afternoon as the pastor went for a walk along the Esplanade. She had seen the way he had looked at the scantily dressed women who came from the beach and she had been certain that it was not their salvation which had occupied his mind. 'But', she said, 'you can't judge the man merely for looking. He's probably a lover of the human body.'

'Lover my ass,' Jomo said as they followed her into the lift which took them to the fourth floor. They walked along the carpeted passage in silence until they reached the door. Zelda knocked.

'Who is it?' a disembodied voice called from inside.

'Doctor Hedges?' Zelda said, winking at the two men. *Doctor*. That was a neat touch. People immediately concluded that you were elevating them above mere mortals, especially in South

Africa. 'I've been sent by the diocese to meet with you.'

'What about?'

'Oh,' Zelda said casually, 'a problem. But I wouldn't care to discuss it here in the corridor. It's kind of . . . private.'

The door opened a crack. A blue eye peered, saw Zelda and then the chain was unlatched. Zelda went in first, followed by Jomo with Mboza taking up the rear. Hedges, a tall man in his fifties, had a boyish face with the merest beginnings of a double chin. His thinning steel-grey hair was tousled, which meant he must have been enjoying an afternoon siesta. He registered mild surprise at the two men, but quickly regained his composure.

'I'm sorry we're disturbing your peace, Doctor,' Zelda said, striding to the only settee in the room. She directed Jomo and Mboza to sit on either side of her. In this way, Hedges was forced to perch on the edge of the bed. 'But we've been having this problem and I have sought help far and wide. And then I heard about you.'

'What kind of problem?' Hedges's eyes moved from Zelda to the men, then back to her, to her legs which crossed and uncrossed at intervals.

'Can I use your toilet?' Mboza asked, jiggling his legs like someone who really had to go. Hedges hardly looked at him. 'Over there. Close the door.' He indicated the bathroom with the jerk of his head. Then he leaned forward, his elbows on his thighs with the fingers forming a pyramid under his jaw. 'What's the problem?'

Zelda looked uncomfortable. 'Well,' she started, shooting Jomo a quick glance, 'it's about him, really. We've been going out together . . . ' She gave a small embarrassed laugh. 'It's nothing. We haven't known each other that way . . . you know?'

'Sexually, you mean?' Hedges prompted, unloosening his top shirt button. 'Go on, child, I'm used to hearing confession.'

'I thought you would be,' Zelda said. 'Thing is, even though we haven't slept together, he's been wanting me to do . . . things.' From where they sat, Zelda and Jomo could see wisps of white smoke coming out of the bathroom. 'Wrong things. Unnatural acts.' This last she said in her little-girl-lost voice.

For the first time, Hedges registered an interest in Jomo. He looked at him, the blue eyes boring into his as if trying to fathom the depth of the black heart which wanted such a nice white girl to do wrong things. 'Like what?' he asked, turning to Zelda.

'First of all he tempts me,' Zelda said, crucially mortified by her own confession, running her hands along her thighs, her eyes on Hedges, 'and gets me so hot that I think I should sleep with him. But then I'm a good girl, and my parents taught me right.'

By now the smoke was all over the room. Hedges seemed uncomfortable, shifting his position on the bed. As Zelda spoke of Jomo's depravity, how he tied her up and hit her with a belt across the buttocks, Hedges's eyes had started to glaze. 'Yes,' he said. 'I'm familiar with that phenomenon. We have to be strong against the wiles of the Evil One.' He turned his eyes to Jomo again, this time making a positive identification of the real representative of the Evil One in this splendid hotel.

'But what's bothering me is that I find myself actually enjoying this . . . '

Jomo got to his feet. 'I'm sorry,' he said. 'You'll have to excuse me, but I can't sit here and have my private life discussed like this . . . '

Hedges didn't even acknowledge his presence. 'Go on,' he said.

On going out, Jomo ensured that the door wouldn't latch. Mboza followed. The two men stood with their backs against the wall, smoking. 'How many minutes?' Jomo asked.

'I don't know,' Mboza said, 'because I cooked a big bomb in there.'

'What do you mean you don't know?'

'Well, it differs from person to person.' Mboza said. 'For instance, someone who hasn't been with a woman for a long time will go absolutely ape the minute he gets a whiff of the *muthi*.' He took a long drag of his cigarette. 'Also, I don't know whether this thing works on white people. I've never had a chance to test it on them.'

'But if it works on Hedges,' Jomo asked, 'is she going to be safe?'

'She looks like someone who can take care of herself,' Mboza said. 'She must have used mace before. White women could teach you a thing or two about mace and pistols.'

They listened to the hum of the air-conditioning and the discordant squawks of the seagulls outside. Somewhere in one of the rooms a couple were arguing heatedly; from another room came the sound of a Western on television, the guns popping off. Just then they heard a dull thud, and then the sound of bare feet on the floorboards. Then there was Zelda's voice, disjointed, 'No,' she was saying, 'not like that . . . let me help you . . . ' Then the stertorous breathing. Hedges. Then there was silence. After a long while the door opened and a flushed Zelda stuck her head out. 'Come on in,' she said. 'Help me carry him to the bed.'

They entered and found the room looking as if it had been hit by a hurricane. The side lamp was on the floor, the bedding was in disarray. Hedges, stripped down to his shorts, lay propped against the bed. He was breathing softly but regularly. They lifted him and took off his shorts. Then Zelda handed Jomo a scarlet pair of Pleasuredome panties. When they had dressed the unconscious man, they fastened a matching brassiere across his chest. Having laid him spread-eagled on the bed, they secured his arms and legs with handcuffs.

Zelda then opened her bag and took out some cosmetics. 'Now the creative part starts,' she said. Very carefully, she dabbed his face with foundation cream, powder, rouged his cheeks, applied eye-shadow, mascara and eye-liner and exaggerated his lips with lipstick. She stepped back to admire her handiwork. 'Oh,' she said, 'we mustn't forget the hair.' Whereupon she lifted his head and covered it with a costume wig. It was brown, Jomo had to marvel at her thoroughness. She was true to form to the bitter end.

Reaching into Mboza's bag, Jomo took out a Polaroid camera. He took a picture. They waited for the print to dry. Then Jomo took another one and pocketed it. On the back of the colour photo, he scrawled the message:

Dear Reverend Doctor Sir
There is nothing personal in this, but this is just to tell you to get

145

*off people's backs. We want to make mistakes on our own terms. You've
caused my father a lot of pain, and caused him to doubt himself as a
man and I just want you to let him lead his folk without your fucking
with him.*

Cheers
Jomo Khumalo.

When the day for the baptism at Horizon neared, Khumalo, the
chief deacon, summoned his son to hear what had transpired
with Hedges. He had hoped that Jomo would have enlisted the
help of his powerful white friends and put in a good word for
him. But when Khumalo heard what had happened, he nearly
had a stroke. He told his son that he never wished to see him
again. Jomo, not wanting to let their effort go to waste, decided
to go ahead and finish what his father had started. He wore his
father's robes and borrowed Hedges's name, happy that the
man had taken the first available flight back to England.

Zelda continued, in a loose and unstructured way, to play a
part in his life. For her, it had been an eye-opening experience,
and she would tell the story of a man who was taken from his
holy perch by African herbs and brought to the ground where
he wanted to act like a man. She still wondered loudly what
would have happened if they hadn't armed her with mace, because Hedges's passion had been real and, at one point, almost
overpowering. Jomo stopped taking her calls when she said she
wanted to know Mboza better. His uncle, he knew, would drive
her into a madhouse.

Now, as Jomo went down with the converts in the small Horizon river, he felt a joy he had never experienced before. The water
washed over him, over them, while the celebrants sang, glorify-
ing their God as they stood on steady ground. Even Dlamini
was to comment later that the young deacon was the real McCoy,
he was in touch with the people and knew the currents and the
crucial moment to immerse into the healing river and purify
the sinners who had turned their backs on iniquity. Underwater, the only place where Jomo wished to be, he was able to
see visions which he stored in a vault in his mind. These would
later become images that the world would see at the moment of

his rising, here, in this place with a strange name. He would paint pictures that had lain submerged in his mind and gladden the hearts of young artists who needed inspiration and hope. He knew, then, as he invoked the Holy Trinity that the water had finally irrigated the barren field in his soul and he had found the inspiration, a direct line to his own, personal god.

Africasouth New Writing

The Africasouth New Writing series aims to introduce new authors who have not yet established a following, and also includes works published for the first time by well-known writers.